THE GREAT GRAIN ELEVATOR INCIDENT

KEVIN MILLER

MILLSTONE
PRESS

Kevin Miller/Millstone Press
Box 380
Kimberley, BC, Canada V1A 2Y9

www.kevinmillerxi.com
www.facebook.com/MilliganCreekSeries

The Great Grain Elevator Incident/Kevin Miller. -- 1st ed.

ISBN: 9781694075376

Cover illustration by Kierston Vande Kraats (https://kenriots.carbonmade.com)

Dedication

For Foam Lake, a little town with a strange name that still holds a dear place in my heart. My days there weren't always happy, but over the long haul, the good certainly outweighs the bad.

CONTENTS

1

DEMOLITION

The old wooden grain elevator loomed like a lonely sentinel under the pale-blue autumn sky. In spots where its maroon paint had peeled away, its shiplap siding had turned gray, and the name of the community where it stood was barely legible on the building's side, though it had once been visible from a great distance in big yellow letters.

"Are you sure the batteries are fully charged?" thirteen-year-old Matt Taylor asked as he hovered over his friend, Andrew Loewen, a curly-haired, self-taught mechanical genius and one of Matt's best friends.

"Yes, for the tenth time," Andrew replied as he adjusted the focus ring on one of two video cameras that the boys had set up to capture the monolith's imminent demise.

For the better part of a century, the grain elevator had faithfully served the village of Roosevelt, Saskatchewan. Standing tall through all kinds of weather, it had witnessed years of optimism and hope, and days of mourning and despair. It had presided over parades, funeral processions, wedding celebrations, and even the occasional crime, although nothing too terrible ever happened in Roosevelt. But despite its years as a focal point for local farmers, a place where they not only unloaded their grain but also caught up on gossip and curling scores, today the elevator's abiding presence was about to end.

"It sure is a shame to see the old girl go," Matt said, snapping a photo of Andrew as he hunched over the camera to make a few last-minute adjustments.

"We've all gotta go sometime," Andrew replied. "Besides, you can't stand in the way of progress."

Matt sniffed in disdain. "You sound like my dad. Bigger isn't always better, you know." He looked toward the shimmering outline of the nearly complete inland grain terminal being constructed in the distance, its image distorted by heat waves rising from the warming ground. "I don't care how much money it saves Fortitude. That thing is ug*ly*."

Like so many other wooden grain elevators over the past decade, Roosevelt's elevator had been declared redundant due to the enormous cement-and-steel inland terminals that big grain-handling companies like Fortitude were erecting across the prairies. Though the terminals were far more efficient, they were bleak and gray and triggered none of the romantic memories of days gone by that the old wooden elevators inspired. Once a grain elevator was demolished, it was as if the community's history disappeared with it. Therefore, Matt was determined to document as many such demolitions as possible, hoping to preserve the elevators' final moments for future generations.

Matt turned back toward Roosevelt's elevator and watched as workers in yellow hardhats finished their preparations around the building's base. The plan was to set off several explosive charges attached to the foundation, causing the elevator to topple onto its side, which would create a spectacular explosion of grain dust and debris, which the boys were in a perfect position to capture on videotape.

"I wonder how the other guys are doing," Matt said. He unclipped a walkie-talkie from his belt and held it to his lips. "Camera two, this is camera one. What's your status?"

The boys' second camera, which was about a hundred meters away, hidden from Matt's view behind a stand of poplar trees, was manned by his brother, Chad, who was one year older than Matt. Assisting Chad was Dean Muller, the fourth member of their tight-knit group. The boys were from Milligan Creek, a small town about forty-five kilometers west of Roosevelt. Andrew's dad had driven the boys to Roosevelt that morning, so they could film the demolition.

"I thought we were camera one," Dean replied over the walkie-talkie.

Matt grinned at Andrew as he keyed the mic. "Just tell me you're good to go. We'll only have ten seconds once they blow the horn, so we need to be ready."

"That's the problem," Dean said. "We are ready, but someone just got in the way of our shot."

"Well, ask them to move."

"It's not that simple," Dean replied.

"Why not?"

"I think you need to come and see for yourself."

"Seriously?"

"Yes."

Matt sighed in frustration and then tossed his walkie-talkie to Andrew. "I'll be right back. If anything happens while I'm gone—"

"I know, I know, start rolling," Andrew replied, clipping the walkie-talkie to his belt.

A couple of minutes later, Matt jogged up behind

9

Chad and Dean. "Okay guys, what seems to be the—what? Channel Six News? They can't park there!"

Dean turned toward Matt as he approached. "Exactly! They couldn't have picked a worse spot!"

"Or a better one," Chad said, looking up from their camera. "Clearly, we know what we're doing." The boys had chosen the location because from there the elevator was silhouetted by the sun. It would make for a dynamic shot when it fell. Not only would the sun be revealed in a blazing flash of light, its rays would illuminate the dust cloud as it sped toward the camera. Thanks to a modification Andrew had made, Chad and Dean's camera would film the sequence in slow motion, making it even more dramatic.

"Why don't you just ask them to move?" Matt inquired.

"Why don't you ask them?" Chad said.

Dean put his hands on his hips and raised an eyebrow. "Yeah, Matt, why don't you?"

Matt turned toward the white van, which was emblazoned with the Channel Six News logo and had a retractable satellite dish sticking out of the roof. "Is Tucker with them?"

Dean held a pen under his chin, pretending it was a microphone. "Live, loud, and on location," he said, imitating Channel Six News' star reporter, Tucker Butker.

Though Tucker was somewhat famous locally, being called upon to serve as a celebrity judge at 4H competitions, pie-eating contests, and beauty pageants, he was more of a legend in his own mind than in real life. No matter how small the story, he reported on it as if the outcome had world-changing consequences, speaking in a deep, sonorous tone that was clearly fake, though most people didn't seem to notice. Tucker clearly saw himself as destined for bigger and better things, his role at Channel Six merely a stepping-stone to a job at one of Canada's national broadcasters. Why the big guns had yet to come calling was anyone's guess, but it was clear that Tucker believed it was only a matter of time.

Matt took a deep breath. "Anyone wanna come with me?"

"Not really," Dean replied. "I already have his autograph. He gives it to me every time I see him, whether I ask for it or not."

"I'll go," Chad said, popping the camera off the tripod and hefting it on his shoulder.

"What are you doing?" Matt asked. "We need to be ready with that thing."

"I am ready," Chad replied, grinning at Dean. "Ready to capture the confrontation of the century."

"Ha, on second thought, maybe I will tag along," Dean said.

Moments later, the boys approached the news crew. It consisted of Tucker, who was wearing his signature blue three-piece suit; a grizzled middle-aged cameraman named Bill, who wore a greasy ball cap and a tan vest bulging with gear; and a short middle-aged female producer named Lucy, who held a clipboard in one hand and a round mirror with a silver frame in the other, which Tucker was using as he hastily applied his makeup.

Lucy squinted at her watch. "Hurry up, Tucker. They could blow the horn at any time."

"Almost finished," he said, dabbing some foundation onto his forehead with a thin wedge-shaped sponge. "Gotta get ridda that shine!" Then he pulled out a can of hairspray and shook it vigorously. "Now all I need is a final spray to batten down the hatches."

11

"Uh, excuse me, sir," Matt said.

Bill looked up from adjusting the camera's on-board microphone and scowled at the boys. "Hey, you kids can't be here."

"But we're just—"

"Looking for an autograph? Don't worry, I always have time for my fans." Tucker smiled as he pushed past Bill and approached Matt, Chad, and Dean, dousing his head with a generous dose of hairspray as he walked. The wind carried most of it straight into the boys' faces, causing them to cough and choke. Oblivious to their discomfort, Tucker tossed the can to Lucy, who bobbled it while also trying to hold onto her clipboard and the mirror.

"Well, what'll it be?" Tucker asked. "An eight-by-ten glossy? A copy of my book?"

True to form, Tucker had already published his auto-biography, entitled *The Tucker Butker Way: How I Made It Big and How You Can Too*. In agonizing detail, it re-counted his less-than-meteoric rise from small-town boy to small-town TV news reporter, though he wrote as if the journey had required him to overcome seemingly insur-mountable odds. In addition to his story, he had boiled down everything he learned along the way into ten sim-ple life lessons, such as, "Looks are everything" and "Five things you should always pack in your lunch."

"Uh, we don't have a photo or a book, sir," Matt said. "In fact, we're not looking for—"

"No problem at all," Tucker replied, grabbing the clip-board from Lucy and ripping off the front page.

"Hey!" she protested. "That's your script for the newscast!"

"No worries," Tucker said, tapping his left temple with his index finger. "I've got it all right up here. Pen?" Lucy sighed, then surrendered hers to him.

"Now, who should I make this out to?" Tucker asked, brandishing the pen with a flourish. "Just one of you or all three?"

"Sir," Matt began again.

"Call me Tucker. That's who I am to all my friends."

"Tucker, Mr. Butker, sir, I'm sorry, but we aren't looking for an autograph. We came here to ask—"

Just then, Tucker spotted their camera. "Of course! You're aspiring young journalists. Budding TV news reporters! You came here looking for advice. How silly of me." He tossed the pen back to Lucy, who struggled to catch it while holding onto the clipboard, the mirror, and the can of hairspray while also trying to catch the paper as it seesawed back and forth through the air on its way to the ground. "Let me see that thing." Tucker held out his hands, motioning for Chad to hand him the camera.

"But sir," Matt said, "I mean Tucker, Mr. Butker, we really don't have—"

"Don't be shy now. There's no need to apologize for your gear, which is obviously less than stellar. But we all have to start somewhere, right?" He took the camera from Chad and examined it. Clearly, he had never handled a camera in his life, but a little thing like that never stopped a man like Tucker Butker. It went along with rule number eight from his book: "If you don't know something, act like you do, and most people won't notice."

"Now let me see here . . . there's the lens, and this must be . . . yes, there it is, the viewfinder. I should probably have Bill talk to you about this. He knows way more about cameras than me. But anyway, if I have this right, you hold it on your shoulder like this and—"

WAAAAHHH!

"The air horn!" Chad yelled. "Ten seconds to demolition!"

"Quick, Tucker, get in place!" Lucy said.

Tucker handed the camera to Chad as Lucy passed him his microphone. "Sorry, boys. We'll have to resume our lesson later. Bill, how's my hair?"

"What do I look like," Bill grumbled as he focused the camera, "a beauty consultant?"

Chad's eyes flew to Matt. "What should we do?"

Matt had already snatched Dean's walkie-talkie off his belt, generating a scowl from his freckle-faced friend. "Hey, what the—"

"Roll, Andy! Roll!" Matt said, ignoring Dean's protest. Then he tossed the walkie-talkie back to Dean and grabbed the camera from Chad.

"Hey, what are you—"

"If these guys won't move, I will," Matt said, putting the camera on his shoulder. "See you on the flip side." With that he ran off, straight toward the grain elevator.

"Hey, kid!" Bill said, looking up from his camera in alarm as Matt charged through the yellow safety tape that had been set up around the perimeter. "You can't—"

"Don't just stand there, you idiot!" Lucy bellowed. "Roll, roll, roll!"

Bill opened his mouth to protest and then shrugged and put his eye up to the viewfinder.

"Are you sure, Lucy?" Tucker asked. "The boy could—"

"I said, roll!" the little woman replied, her face reddening beneath her dyed blond hair, which was pulled back into a harsh ponytail.

The consummate professional, the moment Bill gave

him the signal, Tucker cleared his throat, settled his face into a grave expression, and looked straight into the camera. "This is Tucker Butker, live, loud, and on location for Channel Six News. In a startling development at today's routine grain elevator demolition in the town of Roosevelt, a young, aspiring reporter has put himself in harm's way to—"

BOOM!

Tucker cringed and instinctively covered his head as the charges went off behind him.

"Matt, get out of there!" Chad yelled.

Instead of running away from the collapsing elevator, Matt continued to run straight toward it, still filming.

"Lucy, shouldn't we—"

"Keep rolling!" Lucy yelled, choking off Tucker's question.

"He's going to die!" Dean cried.

"Exactly," Lucy muttered to herself. "And if he does, we'll have it all on film."

A moment later, the elevator hit the ground with a crash, sending up an explosion of wood chips and grain dust. The billowing brown cloud roared across the railway tracks and into the adjoining field, swallowing everything in its path, including Matt.

2

MEDIA SENSATION

"Tragedy struck this morning in the tiny community of Roosevelt," Tucker said, his face mirroring his mournful tone as he looked into the camera. "What was to have been a routine demolition of a grain elevator was marred by the death of an intrepid amateur reporter. Perhaps even more heartbreaking, it seems almost certain that this brave, talented young man was inspired to enter this noble profession, to put his life on the line for the sake of a story, by none other than yours truly. In fact, just minutes before this calamity occurred, he came to me seeking advice, which means I was one of the last people . . ." his voice broke slightly, "to see him alive." He paused to wipe away a tear. "While I pride myself on merely reporting the news and not becoming part of the story, in this case I fear I must make an exception. Alas, it seems the old saying is true: no good deed goes unpunished."

"Perfect," Lucy said. "Keep rolling on that dust cloud, Bill. And Tucker, be ready to record the other script if he survives. Either way, we're running with this story as tonight's lead."

As he awaited the outcome, Tucker walked over and

joined Chad and Dean, tucking a small plastic bottle in his suit jacket pocket, a fact that did not go unnoticed by Dean.

"Were those tears fake?" he asked, leaning over to get a better look at it.

Tucker wiped his eyes. "Probably due to the dust, my boy. They'll go away in a minute."

"But the dust cloud hasn't even reached us yet."

Tucker sighed, ignoring Dean's remark. "What a shame. And he showed such promise too."

Dean looked at Tucker in surprise. "We don't even know what happened to him yet. And you're talking about *his* brother, by the way." He pointed at Chad, whose eyes remained fixed on the dust cloud, which was just starting to lose momentum, though it was still growing. "Show a little sensitivity."

Tucker's eyes widened in surprise. "His brother?" He turned back to his producer. "Lucy, we've got the brother right here!"

"Really?" She waved her clipboard at him. "Get him in front of the camera!"

Tucker turned to Chad. "Young man, I know you're in the midst of a potential tragedy here, but would you mind if—"

"That's it. I can't just stand here."

"There goes another one!" Tucker yelled as Chad took off toward the dust cloud.

"Chad, no!" Dean shouted.

"This is brilliant," Lucy said, unable to believe the story unfolding right before her eyes. "Keep rolling, Bill. Tucker, get in front of the camera!"

"What do I say?" Tucker asked, smoothing his helmet-like hair as he hustled into position.

"Just describe what's happening. And keep those tears ready."

Tucker took a moment to center himself and then looked into the lens. "Is there no end to the pathos, the anguish, the horror? And at the same time, the bravery, the honor, and the self-sacrifice. It's said tragedies bring out the worst in people, but they can also bring out the best, and I can't think of a better example of the latter than what we're witnessing right here today . . ."

The moment Chad entered the dust cloud, he stopped short and gasped for air, pulling his T-shirt collar over his face to serve as a makeshift air filter. "Matt!" he yelled, his voice muffled by the fabric. "Matt!"

As he stumbled forward, he tripped over something. Falling to his knees, Chad felt around on the ground until he realized what it was: a tennis shoe. Matt's tennis shoe. Chad looked around in horror, his T-shirt sliding off his face. "Matt!" he said, coughing as the dust choked his lungs. "Matt, where are you?"

"I'm right here, dummy," a voice said from somewhere behind him. "Where are you?"

Chad leaped to his feet and spun around in circles. Finally, he saw a figure emerge from the gloom. "I'm right here!" He ran toward Matt and hugged him. "Are you okay?

"Hey, easy, you're going to break the camera!" Matt said, pulling away. "Oh, and you found my shoe. Perfect. It fell off when I was running. Here, hold this."

Chad took the camera from Matt and then stared at his brother in disbelief as Matt hopped on one leg and pulled on his shoe, as if it was just a normal day. "Do you have any idea what you just put us through?" Chad asked. "Tucker's on camera right now essentially reading your obituary!"

Matt laughed. "Seriously? That's awesome. But not nearly as awesome as the footage I just captured."

Chad coughed, pulling his shirt over his face again as he looked at the camera. "Oh yeah? You don't think the dust destroyed it?"

"I don't see why it would," Matt replied, standing up and taking the camera back from Chad, the visibility already beginning to improve as the dust settled. "Though the lens will probably need a good cleaning, and I'm sure Andrew won't be too happy with me."

"Andrew?" Chad said. "Forget about him, once Mom and Dad find out what you did, there's no way they're going to let us film another one of these things."

For a moment, the look of confidence on Matt's face wavered. "You have a point there. I never even thought of that. I was too caught up in getting the shot."

"And I was too caught up in trying to save you," Chad said. "Now we're both going to get it."

Both boys fell silent as they pondered how, yet again, their enthusiasm for adventure was about to land them in a heap of trouble. For the moment, probably no one but Dean and the news crew had seen what happened because everyone else was standing on the opposite side of the elevator, their backs to the sun. But when the story aired, the entire province would know about it, if not the country.

Suddenly, Matt's face lit up. "I've got it. Come on!" He started off into the swirling dust.

"Where are you going?" Chad asked. "The other guys are back this way."

"Oh, whoops," Matt said, turning around. "It's easy to get disoriented in here. Anyway, there's no need to worry. I think I just figured out how to turn our 'tragedy' into triumph."

Back by the news van, Dean stared at the dissipating dust cloud, searching desperately for any sign of the Taylor boys. "I can't believe it, two of my best friends gone on the same day."

No sooner were the words out of his mouth than he felt a tap on his shoulder. "Excuse me, son," Tucker said. "I realize this is a sensitive time, but would you care to say a few words on camera? To offer a friend's perspective on this heartbreaking misfortune?"

Before Dean could answer, his walkie-talkie crackled to life. "That was some footage," Andrew said. "How'd it look from your angle? Over."

Dean held the walkie-talkie to his lips. "You're excited about the footage? Didn't you see what just happen—"

"There they are!" Lucy said. "Forget that kid, Tucker. Go, go, go!"

Tucker and Dean both looked up as Matt and Chad emerged from the dust cloud, like characters from a post-apocalyptic movie.

"They survived!" Dean yelled. "They survived!"

"What the heck is happening over there?" Andrew asked.

Dean looked at the walkie-talkie and realized his thumb was still on the "talk" button. "Sorry, I'll tell you as soon as I can. Gotta go."

He ran to meet Chad and Matt, then pulled up short as the dust dissipated enough for him to see them clearly. "Ha! You guys look hilarious!"

"We do?" Matt asked, looking at Chad. Then he laughed. "We do!" Both boys were coated from head to foot in dust, the whites of their eyes practically glowing in contrast to it.

"Excuse me, coming through. Reporter coming

through," Tucker said, pushing past Dean with Bill and Lucy in tow. "Ready, Bill?"

"Rolling," Bill said, the camera on his shoulder.

Tucker turned to face the lens. "As you can see, not one but two brave young men put their lives in harm's way today for the sake of the news, and miraculously, both survived to tell the tale." He turned to the boys. "Tell us, what was it like in there? Did you ever fear you wouldn't make it out? Do your parents know you're here?" He shoved the microphone in their faces, awaiting a response.

Chad was about to reply, but then Matt put his hand over the microphone. "We're happy to answer your questions," he said, "but before we do, perhaps you'd like to take a look at what I captured with this." He held up his camera.

"Oh really," Tucker replied, "and what might that be?"

"Before I tell you that, we need to talk about another subject," Matt said. "And that subject is cold . . . cough, cough . . . hard . . . cough . . . cash."

"Cut!" Lucy said before Tucker could reply. She looked at Matt, her blue eyes glittering with possibilities. "What kind of money are we talking about? And what exactly am I paying for?"

§

"Come on, it's about to start!" Matt said as he and the other boys gathered around the TV in the Taylors' living room that evening.

"What's about to start?" asked Matt and Chad's older sister, Joyce, as she sauntered into the room, ice cubes rattling in her tall glistening glass of iced tea.

The boys looked at each other, not even Dean appearing happy to see her, even though he had been in love with Joyce for as long as the other boys could remember.

"Uh, the news," Chad said. "On channel six."

"But I was planning to watch Growing Pains," Joyce said. "You know I never miss it."

"Yeah, well, would you mind missing the first few minutes?" Matt asked. "Just this once? We'd really like to catch the lead story."

"Why? Since when did you guys care about the news? And no, I don't want to miss the first few minutes. Then there's no point in watching the episode."

"I don't mean to be rude," Matt replied, "but is there ever a point to watching an episode of Growing Pains?"

Joyce was about to smack him, but Chad stepped between them. "What Matt meant to say was . . ." He paused and glared at his brother to indicate his snarky attitude wasn't helping. "We're willing to pay you to miss this episode."

Matt stared at Chad in disbelief. "We're willing to do what? With whose money? I didn't agree to—"

"Pay me?" Joyce asked, intrigued. "How much? And more importantly, why? What did you guys do now?"

"Nothing that need concern you," Matt said, glowering at his brother.

Just then, the newscast's opening music started. Joyce grabbed the remote and pointed it at the TV. "Time's ticking, boys. Either tell me what's up, or we're going straight to Kirk Cameron."

Before the boys could answer, Tucker's face appeared on the screen. "Good evening! I'm Tucker Butker, and this is Channel Six News. Tonight, what was supposed to be a routine grain elevator demolition in Roosevelt turned into a near-death experience for an unidentified young cameraman who put his life on the line to help bring you some spectacular footage." The picture cut to Matt disappearing into the cloud of grain dust as the elevator collapsed. "If you think that's amazing, wait till you see what he captured on his camera . . ."

"Is that you, Matt?" Joyce asked, her eyes riveted to the screen.

"Shh . . ." Matt looked around instinctively, even though he knew their parents were out for the evening playing cards with Andrew and Dean's parents. "Yes, it's me. But Tucker agreed to keep my identity—our identities," he gave Chad a meaningful look, "a secret in exchange for our footage."

"They even paid us for it!" Dean said.

Matt glared at him. "That was supposed to be a secret too!"

"And it'll stay a secret," Joyce said, settling into their dad's La-Z-Boy recliner, a devious grin on her face as she sipped her iced tea. "For the right price."

3

THE CLIMBING TOWER

Two days later, the boys were back at school, still smarting from having to pay off Joyce. They were also still adjusting to the restrictions that school put on their freedom, having enjoyed a particularly eventful summer. However, even though it was mid-September, the weather was still warm, which meant gym classes were being held outside, a welcome bonus.

Adding to their enjoyment was the fact that, over the summer, the school had invested in a new outdoor climbing tower. The wooden structure was fifty feet tall and featured a variety of routes, from beginner to expert, including jut-out sections and inclines that would test even the most experienced climber.

Matt was particularly excited about mastering it, and Chad and Andrew weren't far behind. Dean, on the other hand, wasn't so sure. Not only did he have a fear of heights, especially considering a recent unfortunate incident on the high diving board, rock climbing required a level of trust in the person belaying him, and such trust didn't come easily to Dean, considering all the pranks that had been played on him over the years.

Dean stood at the base of the tower, eyes squinting and neck craned as he watched Matt clamber to the top and ring the bell yet again. Matt let out a victory whoop and then pushed off with his feet, spinning himself upside down, so he could rappel headfirst. Fiona, a new girl in town who had developed a bit of a "thing" with Matt during the summer's epic water war, belayed him to the ground. Matt and Fiona had since decided to be friends only, both of them agreeing they were too young for anything serious when it came to romance.

"That was awesome," Matt said, swinging right-side up as his feet touched down on the crash pad. "Let's do it again!"

"Not so fast, Taylor," said Mr. Karky, their stocky, balding gym teacher. "Not until everyone's had a turn. And what did I say about coming down headfirst? Do it again, and you're off this wall permanently. Got it?"

"Yes, Mr. Karky," Matt said, hanging his head but still grinning.

"And wipe that stupid smirk off your face. Muller, you're up next."

Dean could almost feel his face turn a lighter shade of white as the blood rushed from his head to his feet. "M-me? Why me?" he asked as Matt took off his bright orange climbing helmet and handed it to him.

"Everybody's going to make it to the top of this wall by the time this semester is through," Mr. Karky replied. "And when I say everybody, I mean everybody. Now stop gawking, and put on your gear."

Dean took a deep breath to steady himself as he watched Matt slither out of his harness. "Don't worry," Matt said. "There's nothing to it. I'll be holding onto the rope the entire time, so if anything goes wrong—"

"You're belaying me? Why not Fiona?"

"Like Mr. Karky said," Matt replied as he took the rope from Fiona, "everybody gets a turn. That includes climbing and belaying. Isn't that right, Mr. Karky?"

"Stop trying to suck up, Taylor," Mr. Karky replied, eliciting a few giggles from the other students surrounding them. "And hurry up, Muller. I haven't got all day."

Dean frowned at the harness as he held it in front of him. "I don't even know how to put this thing on."

"Here, I'll help you, Dean," Andrew replied, stepping forward.

Once Dean was all suited up, he stood at the base of the wall and looked up. "Which route is the easiest one again?"

"The green handholds," Andrew said, pointing to them. "Follow them all the way to the top."

Matt scoffed. "Those are for babies. Go for the blue ones at least."

"Green it is," Dean replied, grabbing hold of the first two handholds. "On belay?" he asked, looking over his shoulder as he gave the customary signal to indicate he was ready to begin climbing.

"Belay on . . . I guess," Matt replied, indicating he was ready to begin feeding rope to Dean.

Dean started up the wall, slowly at first and then faster as his confidence grew. "Hey, this isn't as hard as it looks," he said.

"No kidding," Matt muttered. "You're using the kindergarten route."

"You're doing great," Andrew replied, staring up at Dean. "Use your legs as much as possible, so your arms don't tire out."

"Got it," Dean said as he extended his arm to reach the

27

next handhold. "You know, maybe I should have done the blue route. This is almost too easy."

"Don't get cocky," Andrew warned. "You're not even halfway to the top. Just keep climbing, slow and steady, and whatever you do, don't look—"

Before Andrew could complete his sentence, Dean's left foot slipped, and he looked down, frantically trying to find a new foothold.

"—down," Andrew said. But his warning came a moment too late.

Once Dean found a foothold, he froze in place. "Help!"

"Come on, Dean," Matt said as he glanced around, not wanting Dean to embarrass himself in front of the other students. "You're fine. Just keep going. I got you." He tugged on the rope to remind Dean that he was firmly in control.

"I can't!" Dean said. "I'm stuck!"

"Knock it off, Muller!" Mr. Karky stepped forward and glared up at Dean, his fists planted firmly on his hips. "You get to the top of that wall right now, or you'll be climbing your way into detention for a week!"

His knuckles white as he clung to the handholds, Dean slowly turned his head and looked up. "What color is the easy route again?"

"Green!" chorused the other students, who stood in a semicircle at the base of the tower, riveted by Dean's attempt.

"You can do it, Dean!" Fiona said.

"Moo!" said another voice. It came from Ben. He was obsessed with cows. For Ben, the word "moo" was a universal term that could mean everything from "yes" to "more milk please" to "I have to go to the bathroom."

"That's right," Matt replied. "Dean-ie, Dean-ie . . ."

As the other students took up the chant, to Dean's surprise, he felt his confidence grow. Clenching his teeth to steel himself, he finally let go of one handhold and reached for the next one. The movement was met by cheers down below. Emboldened even further, Dean hoisted himself up to the next foothold.

"That's it!" Fiona said. "Keep going!"

His body surging with renewed courage, Dean continued up the green route until he reached the top. Without a moment's hesitation, he rang the bell.

"You did it!" Matt yelled. "Way to go!"

The other students cheered. Even Mr. Karky seemed impressed—sort of. "Don't just sit there," he said. "Get back down here, so someone else can take a turn."

"Okay," Dean replied. Just as he was about to rappel down, he glanced at the highway, which ran along the south side of the school grounds. As he did, he spotted three brand-new white trucks, all of them emblazoned with the green Fortitude logo. When they reached Milligan Creek, they slowed and turned onto a service road that paralleled the highway, then headed west of town.

"That can't be good," Dean mumbled. He glanced down. "Hey, Matt, check out the—" The moment he lifted his right hand to point at the trucks, his right foot slipped, and suddenly he found himself hanging upside down, hands scrabbling to grab hold of the wall. "Help!"

"Don't worry, I got you!" Matt said, slowly lowering Dean, who was still hanging upside down.

When Dean was about six feet from the ground, the rope lurched to a stop. Mr. Karky stepped in front of him, his eyes boring into Dean's as the boy slowly spun around until he was face to face with his gym teacher, though Dean's face was upside down. "Didn't you just hear me tell Taylor no rappelling headfirst?"

Dean's freckles looked like brown islands floating on a red sea due to all the blood rushing to his head as he twisted back and forth, struggling to turn right side up. "Yes, sir, but I didn't mean to—"

"You better love cleaning gym floors as much as you love disobeying, Muller, because that's exactly what you'll be doing for me at noon hour for the rest of the week. That goes for you too, Taylor," he said, turning to Matt.

"Me? What did I do?" Matt asked. "I just got him out of a tough situation."

"And into an even tougher one," Mr. Karky snapped. "Next!"

"Man, that guy is so unfair," Matt said as he lowered Dean to the ground.

"Yeah, well, forget about him," Dean replied as he stood up and unbuckled his helmet. "We've got even bigger problems."

"Oh yeah? What could be worse than five days of mopping Karky's gym floor until it's as shiny as his bald head?"

"I heard that, Taylor!" Mr. Karky said. "Want to make it six days?"

"No, sir," Matt replied, reddening slightly as the other students laughed.

Chad stepped forward and looked at Dean. "What'd you see up there?"

"Fortitude," Dean replied, his face serious. "And they just pulled in to Milligan Creek."

4

A Town in Crisis

"Who cares if Fortitude is poking around town?" Matt said later that afternoon as the boys sat around the table inside the reclaimed MD 500 Defender helicopter fuselage, complete with round bubble windshield, which formed the central part of their tree house. It was located in the shelter belt of trees that surrounded Matt and Chad's acreage. The rest of the structure was made from a hodge-podge of salvaged wood, old windows, and a metal roof. It was an ongoing construction project, the boys constantly adding new features, including bunk beds, bookshelves, a mini fridge, shutters, and window boxes full of flowers, which were Dean's pet project. At the end of the summer, they had added the cab from an old Gleaner combine, which doubled as a sunroom and greenhouse.

"It's a free country," Matt continued. "Besides, Fortitude has two grain elevators here. Why wouldn't they come to check up on them from time to time?"

"They weren't coming to check on their elevators," Dean insisted. "The trucks didn't even stop when they reached town. They just turned onto the service road and kept going."

"See?" Matt said, his face brightening. "They didn't even stop here. So, what's the problem?"

"What if they were heading out to where the seed-cleaning plant is?" Chad asked.

"What if they were?" Matt replied.

"Well, if they're planning to build a grain terminal near town, that's the perfect spot for it."

"Why would Fortitude build a grain terminal just outside of Milligan Creek?" Matt asked. "We have three perfectly good grain elevators in town already."

"Fortitude only owns two of them," Andrew pointed out. "And one of them is pretty old. Farms are getting bigger all the time, and old elevators like that are too small to keep up."

Matt sat back in his bucket seat and nudged an old copy of *Popular Science* magazine back and forth on the table as he thought about the situation. "I still don't buy it. Fortitude would never do that to Milligan Creek. There's no way they'd wipe us off the map."

"Big companies like Fortitude don't care about things like that," Andrew said. "They only care about one thing: money."

"Besides," Chad added, "they wouldn't be wiping us off the map, just shifting things a bit farther down the road. In fact, putting a terminal here means they think Milligan Creek is going to be around for the long haul. It could actually save the town rather than obliterate it."

"Are you kidding me?" Matt said, leaning forward. "Did you see what happened to Roosevelt when they tore down their elevator? And Summerside and Kinsinger and Olson? They all disappeared! Gone, zippo."

"Those towns are still there," Chad pointed out.

"Yeah, but they might as well not be," Matt replied. "Without an elevator, you can drive by without even seeing them. And if people can't haul grain there, it won't be long until people decide they don't want to live there anymore either."

"If we lost our elevators, we'd still have our water tower," Dean said, trying to look on the bright side.

Matt scoffed. "I'm sure they'll find a way to get rid of that too."

"I don't see what you're so upset about," Chad said. "All Dean saw were some Fortitude trucks. We don't even know if anything is happening yet."

"You're right," Matt said, standing up. "It's time we did a little investigating."

§

"I don't know any other way to put it," town comptroller Wally Radom said as he stroked his voluminous black mustache. "Milligan Creek is broke."

"Broke? How can an entire town go broke?" Mayor Michael Bondar asked, squinting at the spreadsheet that Wally had handed out at the start of the town council meeting. Beads of sweat glistened between the strands of hair that stretched from one side of Bondar's bald pate to the other, the product of worry rather than heat. "Haven't people been paying their property taxes?"

"Well, perhaps 'broke' is too strong a word," Wally admitted as he leaned back in his chair. It was one of several black office chairs that surrounded the conference table in the town hall's boardroom. The others were occupied by the heads of various departments as well as the six town councilors, all of whom looked equally perplexed as they examined Wally's numbers. "We have some money in the bank, sure," Wally continued, "but after doing an extensive audit of the town's infrastructure, including required upgrades to water lines, the sewage-treatment plant, storm drains, streets, and parks, not to mention repairs to the civic center, library, and arena, we're drowning in red ink. On second thought, I take that back. 'Broke' isn't nearly strong enough to describe our situation. Perhaps a better word would be, insolvent, indigent, impoverished, impecunious—"

"I get the picture," Mayor Bondar said, growing impatient with Wally's impersonation of a thesaurus. "What I want to know is, how did this happen? And more importantly, what are you going to do about it?"

"How did we get here? You probably know that better than I do, seeing as you've been mayor of this town for close to two decades, and I've only been here for a few months, but let me see . . ." Wally ran a finger down a column of numbers. "Well, there's the ten thousand dollars spent on Percy the Pike, for starters."

"Percy" was the nickname given to a huge fiberglass statue of a northern pike that had stood outside Milligan Creek for over a decade, advertising nearby Lark Lake, which was a fishing hot spot and popular resort area. The sign beneath Percy boasted that he was the largest northern pike in the world—which he was, until a town in northern Wisconsin seized the title, their pike being one foot longer than Percy. The news had prompted a local crisis, with council voting swiftly to add two feet to Percy's tail, thus reclaiming the crown, at least for the moment.

"Those Yankees'll think twice before trying to one-up us again," Mayor Bondar said, generating a chorus of enthusiastic nods and murmurs around the table.

"There's also the fireworks at this year's Milligan Creek Daze celebrations. That was another five grand."

"Five thousand dollars? For fireworks? Who approved

that?" Mayor Bondar asked, his eyes roving around the table until they landed on Carl Gustafson, the town's parks and facilities manager.

"Don't look at me," Carl replied, chewing fiercely on a gigantic wad of gum, which caused his right cheek to bulge. He was trying desperately to curb a nasty chewing tobacco habit, thanks to an ultimatum from his wife. "The council approved the budget."

"Well, they were pretty spectacular," Mayor Bondar admitted.

"Spectacular? They were fantastic!" Carl said. "I'm already planning to double the size of the show for next year."

"Moving on," Wally continued, fearing his warning was falling on deaf ears, "we have the little signs you put in the ditches in the winter to control snowmobile traffic, even though snowmobiles aren't allowed to operate within town limits."

"But the signs are so cute," Mayor Bondar said, "and we haven't had an accident since they went up."

"Then there's the goodwill trip that you and the council members took last year to Milligan Creek's sister city in Japan."

"It was a fact-finding trip too, don't forget," Mayor Bondar said, "for the Japanese garden we're planning to build in Central Park. And we used a provincial grant to help pay for it."

"About that garden," Wally replied. "Two thousand dollars to build a koi pond? Do we even know if koi can survive a Saskatchewan winter?" He looked around at the group for an answer.

"We've funded a study in partnership with the University of Saskatchewan to find out," council member Bob Dancy replied, smiling proudly. Bob also worked as a conservation officer.

"At a cost of another twenty-five hundred dollars," Wally pointed out.

"Don't be so pessimistic," Mayor Bondar said. "Who knows? Perhaps Milligan Creek will become a global center for koi research."

Wally raised a skeptical eyebrow and then turned the page. "Then there's the new Christmas decorations for Main Street, ten thousand dollars. The repairs to the old clock on the post office, one thousand dollars. The new fire truck, one hundred and twenty thousand dollars. And what's this item here, two thousand dollars to bring in a group that recreated Shakespeare's play, Hamlet, featuring a cast of dogs?"

"And it was a barking good time, wouldn't you agree?" Mayor Bondar asked, turning to the other council members, who smiled and nodded in agreement. "Especially that little cockapoo who played the ghost of Hamlet's father. Wasn't he a gas?" He turned back to Wally, who was staring at him in disbelief. The mayor scoffed and waved his hand dismissively. "Well, you're an accountant. What would you know about art? It's highly subjective."

"Do I even need to mention the three thousand dollars spent administering Swedish massage to whitetail deer?"

"The town is overrun with them," Mayor Bondar replied. "They're a menace, and we thought it might have a calming effect. It was a pilot project."

"I could go on," Wally said, tossing his report onto the table, "but rather than get bogged down in details, my point is this: this town has a long history of frivolous spending. That, coupled with aging infrastructure and a shrinking population, has put us over a barrel. Frankly, I'm amazed the situation has been allowed to go on for as long as it has. As for what we can do about it, I don't see any easy solutions. In fact, if Milligan Creek were a person and not a town, I'd advise that person to declare bankruptcy—immediately!" Wally's comments were met by stunned silence as the weight of his words sank in.

"Unless . . ." Everyone looked up at the sound of the voice. It belonged to Theo Hickenlooper, who sat at the far end of the conference table, opposite the mayor.

Theo was the youngest and newest member of the town council, voted in midway through the term to replace another council member, who had to step down for health reasons. He had grown up in Milligan Creek and then left for a few years to get an education and some experience in the wider world. Having had his fill of the big city, he had recently returned to Milligan Creek, setting himself up as an insurance broker. However, more than a few big-city ideas had followed him home, including a penchant for three-piece suits, complete with bow tie. Although the suits, accompanied by horn-rimmed glasses and slicked-back hair, made him look like a banker out of an old movie; rather than look to the past, Theo was all about ushering Milligan Creek into the future, a fact that had already ruffled more than a few feathers around the council room table.

"Unless what?" Mayor Bondar asked, barely able to conceal his contempt for the diminutive and, in Bondar's opinion, arrogant young man.

"Unless we embrace some radical new thinking," Theo said, rising out of his chair. The other council members' eyes followed him as he paced in front of the row of windows that ran along the west side of the boardroom, looking out toward downtown.

"What kind of new thinking?" Mayor Bondar asked.

"Let me put it this way." Theo stopped pacing and

37

turned back to face the group, pausing dramatically to ensure he had their full attention. "I think it's high time this town showed a little . . . fortitude."

§

Matt, Chad, Andrew, and Dean brought their bikes to a stop on the service road just west of Milligan Creek. A few sparrows chirped as they swooped over the recently harvested canola field that surrounded the plant, and a gentle breeze ruffled the stubble, which glowed yellow in the sunlight. Otherwise, there were no signs of life, and no sign of the white Fortitude trucks that Dean had spotted earlier that day.

"If they were here this afternoon, they're gone now," Chad said.

"If they even stopped here," Matt added.

"Why else would they turn onto the service road?" Dean asked.

Before Matt could reply, Andrew pointed at something on the south side of the road, opposite the stubble field. "What's that?"

The boys followed his gaze to a small white marker flag fluttering in the tall grass. It was stuck into the ground on a thin metal wire. Matt threw down his bike and ran across the road, the other boys right behind him.

"I told you something fishy was going on!" Dean said as they gathered around the flag. It displayed the green Fortitude logo. Matt yanked the flag out of the ground.

"I don't think you should do that," Dean warned.

"Oh yeah? Watch me," Matt replied, already headed for another flag, located about ten feet away.

"Hold on a second," Andrew said, causing Matt to

pause and look back. "Dean's right. You probably shouldn't touch those."

"Why not?" Matt asked.

"For starters, they're not yours," Chad replied, running up and pulling out the flag before Matt could. He hid it behind his back as he marked the spot with his foot, so he would know where to replace it.

"Yeah, that and I think they're survey markers," Andrew said. "Look at them all." The boys looked across the grassy area and saw at least fifty more flags laid out in a grid pattern.

"That does it," Matt said, taking off at a run. Before the other boys could stop him, he ran and plucked each flag out of the ground until he had them all in his hand, like a fluttering bouquet of white plastic flowers. He returned to the group, slightly out of breath, and held out his free hand to Chad. "Allow me to complete my collection."

Chad looked at Andrew, who shrugged. "Might as well now that he's pulled up the rest of them."

As soon as Chad surrendered the flag, Matt hurried off and started planting them in the ground.

"What the heck is he doing now?" Dean asked.

The boys watched Matt's frantic activity in confusion. Then an idea struck Andrew, and he ran back up onto the road. He shook his head in begrudging admiration. "Very clever."

"What do you mean?" Dean asked.

"Come see for yourself."

Dean and Chad ran up the ditch and joined Andrew on the road just as Matt stuck the last flag into the ground. Only then did they realize what Matt had done.

"Go home," Dean said, reading the words Matt had just spelled out with the flags. He glanced around worriedly. "I can't believe you just did that."

"And I can't believe Fortitude is trying to wipe Milligan Creek off the map," Matt said, slightly out of breath as he joined the boys on the road.

Chad sighed. "You're leaping to conclusions, Matt."

"Like always," Dean added.

"Am I?" Matt asked. "Andrew said they look like survey markers. What else could Fortitude be doing except making plans to stick one of their big, ugly grain terminals right here where we're standing? And if they do, we all know what that means."

Instinctively, the boys all looked back toward town, where Milligan Creek's three grain elevators shimmered in the late-afternoon sunlight.

§

"And precisely what are you implying?" Mayor Bondar asked, growing impatient with Theo's theatrics.

"I'm not implying anything," Theo replied. "I'm merely stating the facts. As Wally said, Milligan Creek is broke, and Fortitude is the only one that can save us."

Mayor Bondar huffed. "We've already been down this road. Fortitude made their pitch, and the council voted almost unanimously to reject it—your predecessor being the only holdout, as I recall. Not only did they want us to give them the land for free, they asked for tax breaks, road allowances, and all sorts of other concessions, which meant allowing them to put a terminal here would actually cost the town money rather than generate any new revenue. I'm through with these big agricultural companies trying to push around little towns like ours. Milligan Creek can do just fine on its own."

"Except apparently, it can't—at least not under current leadership," Theo said, offering a pained smile. "With all due respect."

"And what's that supposed to mean?" Mayor Bondar asked, his shiny dome reddening with anger.

Theo turned and looked out the window again. "Only that rather than you or the council making this decision, perhaps it's time we put the issue directly to the voters."

"And how, pray tell, do you propose we do that?" Mayor Bondar asked. "Through some kind of referendum?"

"Some might call it that," Theo said. "Others might call it an election. Like the one coming up this fall."

Mayor Bondar glanced around at the other council members and chuckled. "What are you saying, that you plan to run for mayor? Against me?"

Theo turned to face the group and stretched his lips back in a grotesque expression that was probably supposed to resemble a smile, as if he had learned how to do it by reading a book about vampires. "I'm saying the past is about to get run over by the future, and if you or anyone else doesn't want to get crushed under its wheels, I suggest you get out of the way."

5

A Clandestine Mission

Just after midnight, Milligan Creek's three grain elevators towered over the north end of Main Street, the stoic monoliths casting long black shadows in the moonlight. It was a clear, cool autumn evening, warm enough for a light jacket or a sweater but with enough bite to warn of winter's impending arrival.

Within the shadows, four darker shapes slithered across the railway tracks and then sidled up against one of Fortitude's two elevators, seemingly becoming one with the building.

"This is crazy," Dean said, panting. "I don't know why I keep letting you guys talk me into these things." Like the other three boys, he was clad from head to toe in black, including a ski mask that concealed every part of his face except his eyes and nose.

"Because it's fun, that's why," Matt whispered. "And because our town needs our help." He turned to Andrew. "Are you sure you're okay with going up the other elevator alone?"

Andrew nodded, a puff of steam rising from his ski mask as he caught his breath. The boys had taken a circuitous route through town from Dean's house, where they were supposedly spending the night. "Yeah. Dean can stay at the bottom as my lookout."

"What do I do if I see someone?" Dean asked.

"Radio a warning to us, and then get the heck out of there," Chad said.

"But don't run straight home, or you might be followed," Matt added.

"Where should I go then?"

"Anywhere but your house," Matt hissed. "Come on, we already went over this!"

"I know! I just forget things when I'm nervous."

"Wait a second." Chad put a hand on Dean's arm to quiet him. "What's that sound?"

They all paused and listened.

"There," Andrew said. "A jet." The others followed his pointing finger past the pulsing red glow of the aircraft warning light just visible at the top of the elevator to a pair of blinking green and red lights moving against the background of stars, the rumbling of the airliner's engines following in its wake.

Dean sighed with relief. "Let's just get this over with. The sooner I'm back safe in my bed, the better. There's no way my mom's going to be fooled by that mop. And if she finds out we even looked at her precious dolls, never mind touched them, she's going to kill me."

As a precaution in case Mrs. Muller checked on them, the boys had stuffed pillows and clothing under their blankets and used a mop and some of her collectible porcelain dolls to simulate tufts of hair sticking out. To complete the illusion, Andrew had added a recording of heavy breathing playing softly in the background.

Matt took one last look around and then motioned for

the others to get moving. "Okay, let's go. Be sure to radio when you're in position."

As soon as Andrew and Dean ran off, Chad and Matt dashed around to the side of the elevator and then crept up the loading ramp that the trucks used when delivering grain. The main entrance was blocked by two enormous sliding doors secured by a padlock and chain that passed through the D-shaped door handles. However, because the doors ran on tracks along the top, the boys were able to pry them open just wide enough at the bottom, so they could get inside.

Matt grabbed the bottom of one of the doors with both hands and heaved, pulling it toward him. "You go first," he said through clenched teeth. Chad took off his backpack, shoved it through ahead of him, then got down on his knees, turned sideways and squeezed through the narrow opening. The moment he was through, Matt released the door, and then Chad pushed on it from inside. Matt shoved the bow and arrows that he had been carrying through the gap, and then he disappeared inside the mammoth structure.

§

At twenty minutes past midnight, Mrs. Muller couldn't sleep. She tossed, she turned, she tried a different pillow, she even opened the window a crack, but nothing worked. Careful not to disturb her husband, Dennis, who was snoring peacefully, she slipped out of bed and went downstairs, thinking some warm milk would help her settle.

Moments later, she stood in front of the microwave, waiting for it to finish heating her milk as she stared out the window. She stopped it a second before the timer was up, so the beep wouldn't wake up her husband or the boys, who, to the best of her knowledge, were sleeping in Dean's room upstairs. Taking her mug out of the microwave, she blew on it slightly to cool it, took a sip, then headed for the staircase.

At the base of the stairs, she paused. Something near the china cabinet in the living room, where she stored her porcelain doll collection, caught her eye. She was about to investigate when—

"Audrey, no!"

Her eyes snapped back to the staircase. "Dennis? What's wrong?" When he didn't answer, she dashed up the stairs, heedless of the hot milk sloshing out of her mug. "Don't worry, honey, I'm coming!"

§

Only once they were safely inside the elevator did Chad and Matt dare to turn on their headlamps, which were muted by red cellophane taped over the lens. Their skin bristled, and their heart rate jumped when they heard a low cooing sound up above. Suddenly, something plopped onto Chad's shoulder.

"Pigeons," Matt whispered, wiping the pigeon poop off his brother's shoulder with his gloved hand.

Chad wrinkled his nose in disgust. "Just my luck."

Matt looked up, the weak light from his headlamp barely making a dent in the darkness. "If I remember correctly, the man lift is over here," he said. "Come on."

Outside the adjacent elevator, Dean's back was covered in cold sweat. He shivered despite his warm clothing. He looked up, as if he might see what Andrew was doing inside. Initially, he had heard a quiet knocking sound, but since then all he'd heard was the occasional dog barking in the distance.

He checked his watch. Matt had estimated it would take them no more than forty minutes to pull off the job, but they were already behind schedule. Looking up, he shivered again, wishing he had gone inside with Andrew after all. Anything would be better than waiting and worrying about his mother's reaction if she discovered they had sneaked out. What would he tell her?

§

Mrs. Muller burst into her bedroom, her mug half full and her forearm dripping with milk. "Dennis, what's going on?"

Her husband shot up into a sitting position and looked around blearily. "Wh-what? What's happening?"

"You called my name. I was worried something was wrong. Are you okay?"

Dennis nodded as his mouth erupted into a huge yawn. He arched his back in a stretch. "Yeah, I'm okay. Must have been a bad dream. What time is it?" He looked at the clock and saw it was 12:25 a.m. Then he looked at Audrey, noting the milk dripping from her hand. "Why are you up? And what are you . . . drinking?"

Audrey slurped some of the milk off her wrist and then wiped the rest on her ankle-length pink flannel nightgown. "I couldn't sleep for some reason. I thought some warm milk would help, but now I think I might as well just stay up."

"Don't be silly," Dennis said, lying back down and patting her side of the mattress. "Get back into bed, and we can snuggle. You'll fall asleep soon enough and . . ." Before Dennis could complete his thought, he was snoring.

"Hmph," Mrs. Muller said. "So much for that."

§

Inside the first grain elevator, Matt and Chad were crammed into a hand-operated man lift, a one-person elevator that was used to access the highest parts of the building. To operate it, all they had to do was step on a pedal to release the brake and then pull on a rope, which was attached to a counterweight and pulley above. The faster they pulled on the rope, the faster the man lift moved.

"Whoo-hoo! This is fun!" Matt said, his hands a blur on the rope as he pulled hand over hand.

"Quiet!" Chad whispered, trying not to get elbowed in the face. "And not so fast! We don't want the rope to get tangled in the pulley and leave us stranded halfway up."

"Good point," Matt said, slowing down a little. "How will we know when we're at the top?"

A moment later, the man lift lurched to a stop, the rope unable to advance any farther. "Guess that answers your question," Chad said, opening the safety gate that secured them inside.

He stepped onto a platform, followed by Matt. Both boys shone their headlamps around the narrow space, the beams of red light converging on a wooden ladder that ascended into the darkness.

"Last one up's a rotten egg," Matt said, slinging the bow on his back and beginning to climb. "I wonder how Andrew's doing."

Outside the other elevator, shivering from cold and

fear, Dean was wondering the same thing. "What's taking them so long?" he muttered, looking up at both elevators as he hugged himself and rubbed his arms to stay warm.

Dean was so caught in worrying about his friends that at first the headlights coming down Main Street didn't register. It took another second for him to recognize the familiar silhouette of emergency lights on the vehicle's roof.

"The police!" Dean whispered, hitting the dirt. His eyes on the approaching vehicle, he keyed the mic on his walkie-talkie. "Abort! Abort!" he hissed. "Incoming!"

6

PIGS

Halfway up the ladder leading to the roof hatch, Matt and Chad's walkie-talkies crackled with static, a faint voice barely discernible in the background. Chad hooked his right arm around one rung of the ladder as he unclipped his walkie-talkie from his belt. "Come again?" he whispered. He released the talk button and waited for a response. All they heard was another burst of static and the same muffled voice.

"A pork, a pork?" Matt said. "Did he just spot a pig or something?"

"I don't know," Chad said, keying the mic again. "Dean, this is Chad. What's wrong?" All he got in reply was another burst of static. "We must be too far away," he said, "or maybe the elevator's interfering with the signal."

"I knew we should have bought the more expensive radios," Matt said, resuming his climb. "Maybe it wasn't even Dean. Maybe it was someone else using the same channel as us."

"I hope so," Chad said. "I don't like being in the dark like this. Maybe one of us should have stayed on the ground too."

"And miss the chance to climb all the way up here? Not on your life," Matt said. "Hey, I'm at the top. And guess what? It's locked."

"Are you kidding me?" Chad said, his red headlamp shining in Matt's eyes as he looked up.

"Gotcha!" Matt said, flinging the hatch open and revealing a square patch of stars. "Come on!"

Down below, Dean cringed as the police car stopped at the north end of Main Street, only relaxing when it turned right, heading toward the recreation center on the east edge of town.

"What is it? What's wrong?" Andrew's voice blared in the darkness. Dean nearly had a heart attack as he scrambled to turn down the volume on his radio, his eyes on the police car's brake lights, praying they wouldn't turn on.

"False alarm!" Dean hissed. "Keep going!"

§

Having drank what remained of her milk, Mrs. Muller lay on her back in bed and stared at the ceiling, her arms crossed outside her covers. She huffed in frustration. Of all the nights to have insomnia, why did it have to be this one? She glanced at her husband. What gave him the right to keep sleeping like that, like he didn't have a care in the world? Part of her felt like waking him up, just so she wasn't the only one who was miserable.

It wasn't like she had anything important to do the next day, it being a Saturday, but that was the point. She was looking forward to spending the day puttering around the yard and preparing for winter. If she didn't fall asleep soon, she would hardly be able to drag herself out of bed, never mind push a wheelbarrow or pull a rake. Maybe that would be a good thing though. She could sit on the back porch with a cup of coffee and issue orders to Dean instead. She smiled. She liked the sound of that. In fact, maybe she could even get Dean to . . . Zzzzzz.

§

Having emerged through the roof hatch, Matt took a moment to enjoy the view as Chad's head popped up beside him. "Pretty cool," Chad said.

"Tell me about it," Matt replied.

"Can you see Dean?"

Matt leaned over as far as he dared, clutching the edge of the opening as he attempted to peer over the edge of the roof. He pulled out his walkie-talkie. "Hey Dean, can you see us?"

A moment later, Dean stepped out of the shadows and waved. Matt waved back.

"Did you get my warning earlier?" Dean asked over the radio.

"About the pig?"

"No! I mean . . . well, yeah, the pigs. The police. They just drove by."

"Which direction?" Matt asked, looking around.

"They went toward the rec center."

Before Matt could reply, they heard a noise from the other elevator. It was followed by a brief red glow before Andrew turned off his headlamp.

"Right on cue," Matt said, waving at Andrew, who waved back. "I can't see them from here, Dean, but keep your eyes peeled."

He put away his walkie-talkie and then turned to his

brother. "Pass me the bow." Chad passed it up to him, along with an arrow. "You sure that string is on tight?" Matt asked, examining a string tied just behind the arrowhead.

"Yes, we checked it back at Dean's house, remember?"

"I know. Just double-checking. And make sure the string doesn't get fouled up. We may only get one shot at this."

Chad set the spool of string on the roof next to Matt as he nocked the arrow on the bowstring and then looked toward Andrew. "Man, this is going to be a lot harder than I thought." He pulled the arrow back and tried to spot his target, a garbage can lid that they had lined with a thick layer of Styrofoam to absorb the arrow's impact. The plan was for Andrew to hold it up while ducking beneath the roofline to ensure he didn't get skewered.

Matt lowered the bow in frustration. "I can't see it against the black building and the black sky. What should we do?"

After thinking for a moment, Chad pulled out his walkie-talkie. "Andrew, shine your light on the target."

"Are you nuts?" Matt hissed.

Chad held up a hand to silence him, still speaking into the walkie-talkie. "It's the same color as the aircraft warning lights on top of the elevator, so even if someone sees it, they won't give it a second thought."

"Roger that," Andrew said.

A moment later, the brothers saw the light. Matt pulled back the arrow and sighted in once again. "Much better."

"Ready, Andrew?" Chad asked.

"Ready," Andrew replied.

"Here goes . . . nothing!" Matt released the arrow. As it flew, kite string spooled out after it. It kept going and going. And going . . .

"Did we hit the target?" Chad asked.

"Negative," Andrew replied.

Chad and Matt had their eyes on the string, which was still playing out. Finally, it stopped. "Dang," Matt said. "Wonder where it went." He pulled on the string, reeling it in hand over hand until it went taught. He gave it a tug. "The arrow must have stuck into something." He pulled harder. "I hope it's not—"

"Wait!" Chad said, but he was too late. Matt gave the string a vicious yank, and it snapped. "Great," Chad groaned. "Now what are we going to do?"

"We have more arrows," Matt said, already reeling in what was left of the string.

"Yeah, but do we have enough string?" Chad asked, eyeing the spool.

A few moments later, Matt came to the end of it. He also examined the spool. They figured they had enough for at least one more shot.

Chad asked pulled out another arrow. "Want me to try? I did win first place in archery at camp last summer."

"No, that was just a practice shot," Matt said as Chad tied the string to the arrow. "I'll nail it this time."

"And if you don't?"

"I will," Matt said, nocking the arrow and raising his bow. "Just tell Andrew to be ready."

"Ready for round two," Chad said.

"Roger that," Andrew replied. "Ready."

Matt took careful aim and—

"Abort! Abort!" Dean said, his frightened voice coming through loud and clear this time.

Matt was so shocked that he accidentally released the arrow.

"No!" Chad cried, watching the string fly off the spool as he and Matt flattened themselves against the roof to avoid being seen.

"Bingo!" Andrew said a moment later.

"Yes!" Matt raised his fist in triumph, his body still flat against the roof.

"Dean, what's going on down there?" Chad asked.

"False alarm," Dean said. "A streetlight on the corner just flickered. I thought it was headlights."

The other boys groaned. Matt pulled out his radio. "Andrew, is the string still attached to the arrow?"

"Yes," Andrew replied.

"Okay, tie it to something to make sure you don't drop it. Give us a minute, and then we'll tell you when to start pulling."

As Matt held the string, wrapping it around his fist a couple of times to make sure he didn't let go, Chad cut it with a knife. Then he pulled the end of a rope out of his backpack and tied it to the string.

"Make sure it's a good knot," Matt said.

Chad scowled at his overbearing younger brother. "Did you forget I won first place in rope tying too?"

Matt reddened slightly, though in the dark, Chad didn't notice. "Sorry. Just want to be sure."

"What's taking so long?" Dean whispered over the radio. "I have to go to the bathroom!"

"Just go behind the elevator!" Matt said.

"Are you kidding me?" Dean replied. "I'm way too nervous."

Matt shook his head in disbelief.

Chad finished his knot, tied another one for good measure, and then gave it a tug to ensure it was tight. "That oughta do it."

"Ready when you are, Andrew," Matt said. No sooner were the words out of his mouth than the rope started to spool out from Chad's backpack as Andrew pulled on the string.

"I hope it's long enough," Matt said.

"It will be," Chad replied. "Andrew measured it."

Down below, Dean rolled his shoulders, his neck sore from looking up for so long. Just as he was about to badger the others again about what was taking so long, he saw a flash of white up near the top of Matt and Chad's elevator. "I see it!" he exclaimed into his radio. "It's working! It's working!"

"Of course it's working," Matt replied. "It was my idea. We'll be down as quick as we can. Keep your eyes open."

"Roger that." Dean clipped his walkie-talkie to his belt and then rubbed his hands together to warm them. He shoved his hands into his pockets and jumped up and down, anything to get his blood flowing. His bladder felt like it was about to burst. He was about to take Matt's advice when he heard a sound that was so familiar to him, his house not being far from the railway tracks, that he didn't pay any attention to it at first. When it did finally penetrate his consciousness, his eyes went wide with horror.

A train!

7

DOLL FACE

Matt and Chad didn't need Dean's cries of "Abort! Abort!," which still sounded like "A pork! A pork!" once they were back inside the elevator, to alert them to the fact that something was wrong. They heard the train's whistle loud and clear as it reached the crossroads outside of town. They just hoped Andrew had heard it as well.

"Faster! Faster!" Matt said as Chad pulled on the rope to speed the man lift back down to the ground floor.

"I'm going as fast as I can!" Chad replied, systematically pulling hand over hand. "I don't want to get the rope fouled in the pulleys. Then we'll really be hooped."

When they finally reached the bottom, Matt flipped open the safety gate, and they ran for the big sliding doors. However, just as they were about to push the bottom of the doors open to crawl out, they were blasted by the train's headlights as it thundered into the elevator yard, accompanied by the squeal of brakes.

"What do we do now?" Matt asked.

Chad was already pushing on the doors again. "We get out of here before anyone on board sees us."

"What about the guy in the caboose?" Matt asked as

he slithered through the narrow opening.

"Let's just hope he's asleep," Chad replied, handing him the bow and remaining arrows.

Outside, Dean peeked out from his hiding spot between the wooden pillars that supported the elevator's office, which jutted out from the side of the building, about fifteen feet above the ground. He covered his ears at the sound of the brakes as the train's steel wheels flashed by. He was terrified of being caught but too scared to move, and the train was so loud, it made any attempt to communicate over the walkie-talkies useless.

Suddenly, he saw a flash of movement near the loading ramp. It had to be the other guys. Without a second thought, he ran toward it.

Matt and Chad waited anxiously in the shadow cast by the loading ramp as the train ground to a halt. Having arrived on the north side of the elevator, it was blocking their path back to Dean's house.

"When it stops, we go," Chad said.

"Over or under?" Matt asked, referring to whether they should climb up between the cars or crawl beneath the couplings.

"Over," Chad said. "Going under is far too dangerous. If the train happens to back up or lurch forward for some reason, you'll be squashed like a bug."

"Good point," Matt said.

Suddenly, someone leaped down off the ramp and landed beside them. Matt and Chad were about to bolt, until they realized who it was—Dean.

"Geez, you scared the heck out of us," Matt said.

"Where's Andrew?" Chad asked.

60

"I don't know!" Dean replied. "As soon as the train came, I took off." He was practically yelling over the sound of the train's engine, which rumbled loudly as it idled on the tracks. "Hey, what's that?"

They all looked toward the engine, where they saw a light bobbing beside the train. There was no mistaking it; someone was walking alongside the tracks carrying a flashlight.

"Let's go!" Matt said, already running toward the train. He leaped up, grabbed a handle on the side of a boxcar, and vaulted across the coupling to the other side.

"Go! Go!" Chad said, pushing Dean ahead of him.

"What about Andrew? That guy's right near his elevator!" Dead replied as he stumbled forward.

"Andrew's a smart guy. He'll take care of himself. Just go!"

Dean tried to do the same vaulting maneuver as Matt, but he clipped his foot when he jumped and went tumbling into the darkness on the other side.

"Dean! Dean! Are you okay?" Chad hissed. Hearing no reply, and with no time to lose, he broke out of his hiding spot and leapt over the coupling. Moments later the bobbing flashlight illuminated the very spot where he had been hiding.

On the other side of the train, Chad practically landed on top of Dean.

"Ow!" Dean cried.

"Why the heck are you still lying on the ground?"

"I think I sprained my ankle!"

"What? Where's Matt?"

"I'm right here," Matt said, emerging from the shadows and pulling Dean to his feet. "Come on!" He put Dean's arm around his shoulder, and Chad did the same, and together, the three of them limped off into the night.

"What about Andrew?" Dean asked, glancing back as they hurried down the elm-lined street, their faces gleaming with sweat despite the cool night air. They'd ripped off their ski masks in an attempt to cool off. "Maybe we should call him on the radio."

"No!" Matt said as Chad reached for his walkie-talkie. "If he's hiding near the tracks, the sound could alert the railway guys."

"Good point," Chad replied. "Like I said, he's a smart guy. He'll figure it out."

"I hope so," Dean said, "because if he's not at my house by morning, we'll have a lot of explaining to do."

§

Mrs. Muller tossed back and forth in her bed, gripped by a nightmare.

In her dream, a dark stranger had broken into her house, sledgehammer in hand. As he loomed over her, all she could see was the glint of his eyes and his maniacal smile. She covered her face with her arms, thinking it was the end.

Then she heard a crash. She peeked out between her fingers and realized the stranger hadn't come for her after all. He was after something far more precious—her porcelain dolls! When he opened the china cabinet, the fear flushed out of her body, and she leapt to her feet in a rage.

"Don't you dare!"

The stranger turned to face her, his face still in shadow, though his teeth glowed white in the night. Then he raised his left arm and held something in a beam of moonlight. It was her favorite doll, Persephone, a gift from her

Aunt Gertrude and the very doll that had spawned Mrs. Muller's obsessive desire to collect the antique figurines. Worst of all, the monster was clutching Persephone by her long, silky raven hair, which Mrs. Muller had spent hours brushing as a child.

"No!" Mrs. Muller cried as the stranger raised his sledgehammer, preparing to crush the doll's head. "You filthy animal!"

The figure laughed. "Whatsa matter, doll face?"

Just as she was about to lunge forward to stop him, something made her pause. That laugh, that voice, it sounded familiar. In fact, it sounded just like . . .

"Matt Taylor!" Mrs. Taylor cried, sitting up in bed, the dream evaporating from her mind almost as quickly as it had appeared. The only residue that remained was Matt's face, the sledgehammer, and her precious dolls.

She threw back her covers and leapt out of bed, prompting Dennis to sit up straight, cry out in panic, then lie back down and continue snoring.

She raced out of the room, leaped down the stairs— one hand sliding down the railing to control her descent— then hit the ground floor at a run. She burst into the living room and turned on the light, causing her to squint in pain. She flicked it off, realizing the moonlight was bright enough for her to see.

When the black spots disappeared from her vision, there were her dolls, just like in her dream. In fact, the resemblance was so eerie that she glanced at the window to make sure she wasn't still dreaming, but it was intact.

She turned back to the dolls, opening the door of the china cabinet and gingerly removing Persephone from her stand. Mrs. Muller turned the doll over in her hands, carefully inspecting Persephone's hair in particular. The doll looked perfect. They all did. In fact, they almost looked too perfect.

Just then she heard a thump upstairs. "I knew it!" she cried. Carefully replacing Persephone on her stand, she shut the china cabinet and then raced back upstairs. She went straight to Dean's bedroom and flung open the door.

There they were, all four boys, all of them fast asleep. Puzzled, she stood there for a moment and listened to their heavy breathing. Convinced they weren't faking it, she closed the door, careful not to let the doorknob click as she released it. She stood outside for a moment and listened in case they were pretending. Finally, she wandered back down the hall to her bedroom, still convinced something was wrong but unable to put her finger on it.

As she climbed into bed, for the first time that night her eyelids felt heavy, and she could barely stay awake long enough to pull the covers over her body. Maybe it had been just a dream after all. Maybe Matt Taylor wasn't really the monster she imagined him to be. Maybe . . . Zzzzz . . .

8

Presumed Guilty

Late the next morning, all four boys sat around the Mullers' kitchen table shoveling breakfast cereal into their mouths as Mrs. Muller puttered around preparing a cup of coffee. All of them had slept in—including Mrs. Muller—due to their adventurous night. A small TV on the counter was tuned to channel six. When the clock struck noon, the news came on, anchored by none other than Tucker Butker.

"Good morning, and welcome to Channel Six News," Tucker said. "I'm Tucker Butker, filling in for Sandy Reynolds, and here are today's top news headlines. Civic elections across the province are heating up, and the gloves have already come off in many municipalities, with long-time incumbents facing challenges from all sorts of fresh, new faces. However, perhaps nowhere is this competition fiercer than in the small town of Milligan Creek, where an unknown individual, or individuals, staged a daring stunt last night that at least one local is interpreting as a show of support for Mayor Michael Bondar—and a threat of bodily harm directed at his lone opponent."

The boys' heads all swiveled toward the TV as the scene

cut from Tucker to an image of a white banner floating in the wind, stretched between the town's two Fortitude grain elevators. On it were the following words in green spray paint: "Save Our Elevators, Save Our Town!"

"That's so cool!" Matt said, barely able to contain himself.

Dean clenched his teeth and hissed at him to shut up, glancing furtively at his mother, who was also transfixed by the screen.

"No one knows how the individual, or individuals, behind this exploit pulled it off," Tucker continued, "but at least one Milligan Creek resident is convinced he knows why they did it."

The scene cut to Theo Hickenlooper holding an arrow with a string attached to it. He didn't look happy. Behind him was his white Honda Civic hatchback. As he stepped away from it, he pointed to the vehicle's left rear tire, which was flat.

"So that's where it went!" Matt said.

"Where what went?" Mrs. Muller asked, her eyes narrowing in suspicion.

"Oh, the uh, the salt," Matt said, moving a cereal box, so he could grab the salt shaker.

"What do you need salt for?" Mrs. Muller asked.

"Uh . . . I always have salt on my . . ." Matt looked down at his bowl. "On my Alpha-Bits." When Mrs. Muller didn't look away, he had no choice but to sprinkle a bit of salt on his cereal and then take a huge spoonful and shove it into his mouth. "Mmm-mmm good," Matt said, spewing milk across the table as he tried to keep himself from gagging.

Mrs. Muller grimaced and then turned back to the TV. "Gross."

"Quiet," Dean said, riveted to the screen.

"If this is how Mayor Bondar plans to conduct the rest of his campaign, I can assure you, he better get ready for me to respond in kind," Theo said.

"What makes you think Mayor Bondar had anything to do with this?" Tucker asked.

"Why don't you ask him yourself?" Theo replied.

The scene cut to Tucker knocking on Mayor Bondar's door. "That's exactly what I did earlier this morning," Tucker said over top of the image as Mayor Bondar opened his door dressed in his housecoat, his eyes squinting and his comb-over askew.

"Why are you bothering me so early in the morning?" Mayor Bondar asked. "No comment. Now get off my porch!"

The scene cut back to Tucker in the studio. "Clearly, the plot is continuing to thicken in Milligan Creek. Although authorities are just beginning their investigation, I did a bit of digging on my own and discovered that not only is Mayor Bondar opposed to Fortitude's proposal to tear down Milligan Creek's grain elevators and build an inland terminal on the edge of town, he was also a well-decorated archer during his college days, taking top prizes at several competitions throughout Western Canada. A coincidence? I'll let you be the judge of that." The scene cut to an archival photo from a college yearbook of Mayor Bondar smiling as he stood with his archery gear and a trophy.

"Man, did that guy ever have hair?" Matt asked.

"In other news," Tucker continued, but then Mrs. Muller turned down the volume.

"This is outrageous," she said. "To think Mayor Bondar would attack Theo's car with an arrow. What is this world coming to?"

"Seriously, Mom," Dean said, pushing his chair back. "Do

you really think Mayor Bondar would do such a thing?"

"If not him then who? And by the way, what's the matter with your foot?" she added as she watched Dean limp over to the sink with his dishes.

"Uh, nothing." Dean struggled to stand upright. "Probably just slept on it funny."

Mrs. Muller narrowed her eyes. "It didn't have anything to do with that noise I heard in the middle of the night, did it?"

Dean froze in place at her question, as did the other boys, their spoons halfway to their mouths. "Uh, what noise?" Dean asked, his face reddening.

"It was a loud thump, and it came from your bedroom."

"Yeah, that was probably me, Mrs. Muller," Matt said. "I tend to get quite violent when I sleep. Sometimes I even lash out. In fact, Chad can show you some bruises that—"

"That won't be necessary," Mrs. Muller replied as Chad went to lift his shirt. "It sounded like someone fell."

The boys shared a nervous glance. She was dangerously close to the truth. Following their escape from the elevator, Matt, Chad, and Dean had all made it back safely, but Andrew was still missing. As Dean hobbled downstairs to return Mrs. Muller's china dolls—the only person who knew exactly how they should be placed—Chad and Matt tried to raise Andrew on the walkie-talkie. When he didn't respond, they decided to go back out looking for him.

Just when Matt was about to climb out the window, Andrew appeared, startling Matt so badly that he fell over backwards, hitting the floor. Hearing Mrs. Mullers' footsteps, Chad pulled Andrew inside, and then they all leapt into bed before she opened the door—though Dean was trapped downstairs. They didn't even have time to turn off Andrew's recording of their snoring. They all just lay there holding their breath, which was almost impossible for Andrew, who had just run halfway across town. Only once they were sure she was safely back in bed did Dean return and Andrew tell the others what had happened.

It turns out the train hadn't stopped to load up with grain after all. Andrew overheard the engineer say they had received a signal that a wheel bearing on one of the grain cars was running hot, so he stopped to check it. The bearing happened to be right across from where Andrew was hiding. At the last second, he had found a large sheet of cardboard that had blown into the ditch and pulled it over himself. He was so close to the tracks that the engineer even stepped on the edge of the cardboard at one point. Only when the train started to crawl forward did he make a run for it, leaping between cars on the slow-moving train. The other boys were in awe of his quick thinking and his close brush with the authorities.

"I may have fallen out of bed," Dean said to his mother. "Maybe that's how I hurt my foot."

Mrs. Muller sniffed in disbelief. "Never heard that one before. If I didn't know better . . ." She glanced at the china cabinet in the living room and then shook her head. "Aw, never mind." She headed for the back door. "If anyone's looking for me, I'll be in the backyard."

The boys waited until they heard the screen door slam behind her. Then they all began talking at once in hushed tones, in case Mrs. Muller was listening outside.

"Are you kidding me?"

"This is crazy!"

"Mayor Bondar is going to kill us if he finds out!"

"Who cares about him? We could all get arrested!"

The moment those words were out of Dean's mouth,

the boys all fell silent. Before anyone could respond, they heard the screen door bang again, and Mrs. Muller re-appeared. Their faces reddened, all of them certain they were about to be busted.

"Forgot my coffee," she said, grabbing her travel mug off the counter. She took a sip and was about to head back out when she stopped, eyeing the boys' solemn faces. "Sheesh, talk about glum. How late were you boys up last night anyway?"

"Uh, not too late," Chad said quickly.

"Well, you should get outside and get some sun. You all look like you're about to be sick."

With that, she went back outside once again.

"What would they charge us with?" Matt asked the moment he was sure she was out of earshot.

"Oh, let's see," Dean said, marking each answer on his fingers as he reeled them off. "Trespassing, break-and-entry, reckless endangerment, and that's just for starters."

"I knew you should have let me shoot that arrow," Chad said.

Matt turned on his brother. "As if you would have hit the target the first time! It was so dark, it's a miracle I hit it at all."

"There's no sense pointing fingers," Andrew said, his rare contribution prompting the other boys to fall silent. "What's done is done. If we don't tell anyone it was us, there's no way they can prove anything."

"But they're blaming it on Mayor Bondar," Dean said. "It could cost him the election!"

"Yeah, and all because of us," Matt said, his spoon clattering to the table. "He was our only hope of saving our grain elevators, and now we may have just taken him out of the running."

9

TABLES TURNED

"All right, all right, everyone please settle down!" Mayor Bondar said, pounding his gavel on a long folding table, which sat on a stage at the front of Milligan Creek's community hall. He had convened an emergency meeting on the Monday following what was now being referred to as the "arrow incident," seeking not only to clear his name but also to allow residents to voice their views on the increasingly contentious inland grain terminal issue. As much as he had tried to put it in the rearview mirror, it was emerging as the central issue of the upcoming civic election, threatening to divide the town—and cost him his position as mayor.

Despite Mayor Bondar's protests, the packed hall continued to buzz with angry and excited voices. He was about to pound his gavel again when an amplified voice cut through the uproar. "You heard the mayor, people, simmer down."

All eyes turned to the stage as Theo Hickenlooper, carrying a wireless microphone, strode out to join Mayor Bondar and the rest of the council members, the grumbling fading to a murmur. If Theo had learned one thing in the big city, it was how to make an entrance.

"That's better," Theo said. "Now, before we get started, let me be the first to apologize to Mayor Bondar for my appearing to make unfounded accusations against him on television over the weekend. When I discovered the arrow, which I'll be the first to admit could have just as easily hit an innocent bystander—such as a pet or, heaven forbid, a child—instead of my tire, I was shocked and angry at such reckless endangerment, and I reacted in the moment, as any one of you might have done in my situation. But my behavior was inexcusable, especially considering the ramifications if my accusation is proven correct. I apologize for leaping to conclusions before the evidence is in."

Mayor Bondar opened his mouth to reply but then paused. By all appearances, Theo had just offered an apology, but the more Bondar thought about Theo's statement, the more he realized all Theo had done was double down on his accusation. The arrow could have hit pet or a young child? Seriously? In the middle of the night? The meeting had hardly even begun, and the conniving little sneak was already undermining his authority! Well, Michael Bondar hadn't held onto his seat as mayor of Milligan Creek for nearly twenty years because he was afraid of getting his hands dirty. If Theo wanted to play rough, Bondar was more than ready.

"I accept your 'apology,' if that's what you want to call it, Mr. Hickenlooper," Mayor Bondar began. "If people want to know the truth, it's that you slandered me on television, potentially causing irreparable harm to my reputation—at least that's what my lawyers tell me."

At the mention of the word "lawyers," Theo blanched, the color of his face blending with his starched white shirt collar.

"I say 'potentially,'" Bondar continued, "because anyone who knows me and who is familiar with my long tenure as mayor of this fine town realizes just how ridiculous your accusation is. By way of demonstration, a show of hands, please, can anyone here point to a time where I have ever settled a dispute—either professional or personal—by way of bow and arrow? Anyone? Anyone? Bueller? Bueller?" He smiled when his impression of Ben Stein's character in *Ferris Bueller's Day Off* generated a few chuckles. It always did, though some of the smiles looked pained.

"Of course not. However, I can confirm, thanks to the work of intrepid journalist Tucker Butker," he paused and nodded to the Channel Six News crew, who were filming at the back of the room, causing many people to turn their heads in that direction, "that word of my prowess as an archer has not been exaggerated. In fact, whether or not I'm reelected as mayor this fall, I plan to dust off my bow and put on an archery demonstration at next summer's Milligan Creek Daze. In a show of good faith, perhaps Mr. Hickenlooper might even see fit to do the old apple on the head trick. Whaddaya say, Theo?" He leaned forward, so he could look down the table at Theo's reddening face while humming the William Tell Overture. It generated more laughter from the audience, some of it even genuine.

"With all due respect, Mr. Mayor—"

"But I didn't call this meeting to talk about archery," Bondar said, cutting off Theo's protest. "I called it to talk about this." He nodded to someone offstage. In response, two uniformed members of Milligan Creek's volunteer fire department walked out carrying a white bundle of cloth. They unfurled it across the stage, revealing it to be the banner that the boys had strung up between the elevators, bearing their spray-painted message: "Save Our Elevators, Save Our Town!" It looked to be made of several white bedsheets sewn together.

"First of all, let me thank you gentlemen for retrieving this for us, showing once again what a great purchase our new fire truck was for the town—one of my key promises during the last election, as you might recall."

"Mr. Mayor, I hardly think now is the time to—"

"However, as much as I might agree with this message," Bondar continued, talking over Theo once again, "let me state publicly that in no way do I endorse such tactics or the people behind them. I fully support the efforts of Staff Sergeant Romanowski and the RCMP as they seek to track down the suspects." He nodded at Romanowski, who was seated in the front row. Romanowski nodded back, his thick RCMP-issue mustache bristling as he pursed his lips in determination.

"In fact," Mayor Bondar continued, "let me take this opportunity to ask anyone who has any information that might lead to the capture of the perpetrators to pass it on to Staff Sergeant Romanowski at their earliest convenience."

At the back of the hall, Matt, Chad, Dean, and Andrew sank down in their seats, having arrived late. They glanced around furtively as everyone else also stole a look at their neighbors, wondering who the culprit could be. The boys felt as if every eye was staring at them.

"As you might recall, a short time ago, Fortitude made a pitch to our town, offering to build an inland grain terminal on the west side of our community. On the surface, the proposal sounded great—jobs, economic growth, a chance to put Milligan Creek on the map as a community that embraces the future rather than clings to the past. But upon further examination, their proposal contained none of these things. The jobs would mostly be short-term, during the construction phase only. And when it comes to economic growth, once all the concessions were accounted for—tax breaks, road allowances, and land—it would put Milligan Creek at a net loss, a deal they wanted to lock us into for the next ten years. As I told the council after we voted almost unanimously against the proposal, I'm through with big agricultural companies trying to push around little towns like ours. We don't need Fortitude. We already have plenty of our own—fortitude, that is. Can I get a witness?"

His declaration was met with applause and roars of approval.

"Now that I've spoken my piece, I'd like to open it up to the floor. We have a couple of mics on either side of the room, so if anyone would like to—"

"If I may be so bold," Theo said, smiling as the mayor scowled at his interruption, "now that one of the candidates in this fall's upcoming election has monopolized the floor, perhaps it's time for the other candidate to do the same."

Mayor Bondar opened his mouth to protest, but Theo continued before he could get a word out. "I couldn't agree more with Mayor Bondar in regard to the courage, strength, resilience, and ingenuity that characterize the good people of this town. But that is where our agreement ends. It's also why I feel the need to come clean with you all about the dire situation Milligan Creek is currently facing. Wally?"

He nodded at the town comptroller, who held up a remote control and clicked it, causing a slide to project on the wall behind them. It showed a graph of Milligan Creek's infrastructure costs rising and its tax revenues falling. "As you can see, over the past two decades of Mayor

Bondar's tenure, Milligan Creek's financial situation has gone from bad to worse. And if present circumstances are any indication . . ." He nodded for Wally to advance to the next slide, which painted a dire picture of the town's prospects as it projected its financial situation several years into the future. "Milligan Creek's prospects look bleak indeed." Wally advanced to the next slide, which showed a tombstone and the words "RIP Milligan Creek" and the date "1882–?" written on it.

Mayor Bondar leaped to his feet, squinting as the light from the projector shone in his eyes, overlaying him with the image of the tombstone—an insinuation of doom that he would have gladly done without, had he realized it was happening. "This is outrageous! Wild pontification about the future is no substitute for a solid grounding in the facts."

"You want facts, Mayor Bondar? I'm more than happy to provide them to you and everyone else here." Theo nodded toward the back of the room. "If you would."

Mayor Bondar squinted and shielded his eyes with his hand as he attempted to see who Theo was talking to. Finally, he sat down, so the light from the projector was no longer blinding him, and saw volunteers passing bundles of paper to people at the end of each row. Each person took a copy and then passed it on.

"What my assistants are handing out to you right now is a detailed assessment of the graph that Comptroller Radom just shared with you," Theo said. "Feel free to flip through it now or read it when you get home. Either way, it should become apparent immediately that fortitude, though an admirable quality, is no substitute for reality. In fact, our self-reliance, our ability to weather adversity and persevere through all sorts of difficulties on our own may be the very thing that has blinded us to the truth. And the truth is, no matter how strong, brave, resilient, and determined the people of Milligan Creek are, without immediate, drastic change, this community is doomed to fail." Theo's proclamation was met by stunned silence, accompanied by the sound of pages flipping as people looked through the report.

At the back of the room, the boys' faces reflected the gloomy atmosphere that had descended upon the meeting. Even Matt had to admit the situation looked dire.

"But I could hardly call myself a good citizen, much less a potential leader of this noble community, if all I did was sit up here and identify the problem," Theo said. "I have also taken it upon myself to offer you a solution. Gentlemen, if you will."

He nodded to the side of the stage. A moment later, Mayor Bondar's mouth fell open as two men stepped out, both of them wearing white jackets emblazoned with the unmistakable green Fortitude logo.

10

You *Can* Stand in the Way of Progress

"I can't believe Hickenlooper would pull a stunt like that," Matt said after school the following day. He leaned on the window of the Gleaner combine cab and stared out at the trees that made up the shelter belt surrounding their yard. Their leaves and branches danced in the wind under a slate-gray sky, the weather as gloomy as Matt's mood.

He turned back to face the other guys, who were seated around the table in the MD 500 Defender helicopter fuselage. "I mean, talk about trading short-term gain for long-term pain. I admit the new offer those Fortitude guys made sounded great, but with big companies like that, you know there's gotta be a catch somewhere. They don't do anything unless it benefits them."

"Maybe so," Chad said, "but there is such a thing as win-win, you know. And like Theo said, you can't stand in the way of progress."

"Progress?" Matt pushed off from the window, which was streaked with the first drops of rain, and walked over to join the other boys. "You call tearing down our town and building a monstrosity right down the road progress?"

Chad sighed. "We've been over this before. They're not tearing down our town, just a couple of old grain elevators. As for the 'monstrosity,' I think those new inland terminals are pretty cool—totally high tech. In fact, I may even apply for a job when they start the cement pour. I heard they'll be doing it non-stop for twenty-four hours a day until it's finished, so they'll need a lot of help."

"Really?" Dean said. "How much do they pay?"

"I don't know," Chad said, "but it'll probably be pretty good. Fortitude has some deep pockets."

"Wow, maybe I should apply too. Do you think they'd hire a thirteen-year-old?"

Chad shrugged. "You can always ask."

Matt stared at Dean and his brother, unable to believe his ears. "Are you kidding me? Are you falling under Hickenlooper's spell too?"

Chad opened his mouth to respond, but Andrew beat him to it. "I hate to say it, but Matt has a point."

Dean's eyebrows shot up as he and Chad gazed at their curly-haired friend in wonder. "He does?"

"Don't sound so surprised," Matt growled.

"I know I've been skeptical of Matt's resistance to the terminal too," Andrew continued, "but I've been thinking about it a lot lately, and I've changed my mind. An elevator's not just a place where farmers drop off their grain. It's where they connect, where they share news and farming tips and shoot the breeze. Ever since I was a little kid, it's been one of my favorite places to go with my dad. While we're waiting in line to unload our grain, we go into the office, have a cup of coffee—"

Dean's eyes widened. "You've been drinking coffee since you were a little kid?"

Andrew scowled. "No, but that's beside the point. With the new terminal, most farmers won't haul their own grain anymore, unless they can afford to buy a semi, which most farmers can't. They'll just hire out that part of the job instead, at least to begin with. As grain terminals get bigger, so will the farms, because the big guys can do things cheaper than the little guys. Eventually, the smaller farmers will realize they can't afford to stay in the game, so they'll sell out to the big operations. The farming equipment will also get bigger and more efficient, requiring fewer people to operate it, which means fewer people living out on the land. All that to say, the bigger and more efficient farming becomes, the quicker the community that exists around every grain elevator across the prairies will disappear, not to mention the entire way of life we're enjoying right now."

"You mean the way of life *you're* enjoying right now," Dean said. "I live in town, so—"

"Who do you think supports the town financially?" Andrew asked. "What if there aren't any farmers left to buy groceries or vehicles or send their kids to school or play hockey—"

"Or hire your dad to wire their shops or barns?" Matt added, giving Dean a meaningful look. Dean's father was an electrician who serviced a number of farms and businesses in the area.

"Exactly," Andrew said. "It's a domino effect."

The boys fell silent, listening to the rain patter on the tree house roof. Then Dean heaved out a huge breath. "That sounds depressing. I was planning to live in Milligan Creek for the rest of my life."

"Tell me about it," Matt said, sinking into his chair. "If Fortitude has their way, we'll be lucky if Milligan Creek still exists by the time we graduate, never mind by the time we have families of our own—thanks to short-sighted people like Chad."

He glared at his brother, whose eyes were fixed on the table in front of him. Finally, Chad looked up. "All right, all right, I get it. What Andrew says makes sense. But seriously, how can a few kids stop a huge company like Fortitude? If anything, our stunt just made things worse. You heard what Hickenlooper said at the meeting. It just proved the elevators are a menace and need to be torn down as soon as possible."

"We may not be able to do anything on our own," Andrew said, "but we know someone who can."

All eyes turned to the curly haired genius. "Who?" Dean asked.

"Mayor Bondar."

Matt scoffed. "That chrome dome is toast. You saw him up there. The minute the Fortitude guys stepped out onto the stage, he knew he was hooped."

"No, he was Hickenlooped!" Dean said, holding up his index finger and smiling at his own brilliance. "Get it?"

"Unless . . ." Andrew continued, ignoring Dean's brainwave.

"Unless what?" Chad asked.

"Unless we offer to help Mayor Bondar get reelected."

Matt laughed. "And here I thought I was the one with the crazy ideas."

"I hate to admit it," Dean said, "but Matt's right."

Matt threw his hands up in exasperation. "What's with everyone hating to admit I'm right?"

"My point is," Dean continued, "what do we know about politics? And why would Mayor Bondar accept help from a bunch of kids?"

"Because he doesn't have a choice," Andrew said, standing up. "Now come on. We've got some work to do."

11

A Sneak Peek at the Future

"What do our poll numbers look like today?" Mayor Bondar asked as he breezed into his office two days after the town hall meeting and sat down behind his huge double-pedestal oak desk. The word "poll" was a bit of a stretch, considering his data-gathering method consisted of his campaign manager, Rudy Bricksaw, standing outside the post office that morning asking people who they planned to vote for, but it was the best they could arrange on short notice.

"Not good, sir," Rudy said, sliding a piece of paper across the mayor's desk.

Mayor Bondar looked down at the paper, scowled, then looked up at Rudy. "This isn't poll data. It appears to be a resignation letter."

"Exactly, sir. Having reconsidered the situation, I have decided to withdraw my services."

"But you only came on board yesterday!"

"I realize that, but life is too short to work for a loser."

Mayor Bondar's nostrils flared. "Excuse me?"

Rudy, a reedy middle-aged shoe salesman with glasses and a wisp of a mustache clinging to his upper lip, reddened slightly. "I'm sorry, sir, that came out wrong. I just meant that—"

"I know what you meant, Rudy." Mayor Bondar sighed and then waved for the little man to leave. "You can go, but don't come crying to me when Milligan Creek dries up and blows away, taking you and your shoe store along with it."

"I won't, sir," Rudy said, heading to the door. "And in all seriousness, I wish you the best of luck."

"Does that mean I can count on your vote?"

Rudy thought for a moment and then shook his head. "No."

Mayor Bondar glowered as Rudy scurried out of his office, then punched the button on his intercom. "Rose, any appointments for this afternoon?"

"Just one, sir. With your campaign manager."

Bondar's eyebrows knit together in confusion. "My campaign manager? You mean Rudy? He just quit."

"Not Rudy, sir. Your *new* campaign manager. At least that's what this young fellow is calling himself. And he's not alone."

Bondar took a deep breath and then let it out in a long, sad sigh.

"Are you alright, Mr. Mayor?" Rose asked.

"Yes, yes," he said, having forgotten the intercom was still on. "Alright, send him in—send them in—whoever they are. Thank you."

Moments later, he was surprised to see Matt, Chad, Andrew, and Dean enter his office.

"Excuse me, boys, to what do I owe the—"

"Pleased to meet you, sir," Matt said. "I'm Matt Taylor, and this is my second-in-command—and my brother— Chad. Andrew Loewen here is our technical advisor, and this . . . this is Dean."

Mayor Bondar shook each boy's hand in turn, still not quite comprehending the situation.

"Hey," Dean whispered, pulling Matt aside, "why didn't you assign me a position?"

"Because you're our . . . wild card," Matt replied. "Our ace in the hole."

"Oh," Dean said as he shook the mayor's hand and forced a smile, not quite sure if Matt's explanation was an insult or a compliment.

"It's a pleasure to meet you all," Mayor Bondar said, "but do you mind explaining why you're here?" He chuckled. "Rose said one of you claimed to be my new campaign manager."

"That would be me, sir," Matt said, stepping forward. "We heard you had an opening in that department, so we thought we'd save you the trouble of placing an ad."

"But how did you hear . . . I mean, I only just found out—"

"Word travels fast, especially bad news. Isn't that right, Mr. Mayor?" Matt said as Andrew and Dean set up a portable whiteboard behind him.

"Yes, but—"

"And I can't think of worse news than what happened the other night at the town hall meeting. We've done a bit of research," Matt nodded to Andrew, who put up a line graph showing Mayor Bondar's declining popularity rating over the past forty-eight hours, "and we put your odds of winning the upcoming election at approximately . . . zero."

Andrew put up another graphic, showing the mayor's actual odds to be 0.01 percent.

"I don't understand," Mayor Bondar said. "How did you calculate—"

"The details aren't important," Matt said, talking quickly to keep the mayor off balance. "What matters is the big picture. And what the big picture is telling me—telling us—is your reign as mayor of this town is about to collapse, just as surely as our elevators are coming down if Theo Hickenlooper gets his way."

Andrew put up a drawing of Theo laughing as Milligan Creek's elevators were demolished. Beside it, Dean made the sound of an explosion with his mouth while slowly moving his hands out in front of him to help Mayor Bondar envision the spreading dust cloud.

"These are dark days indeed, Mr. Mayor," Matt said, continuing his pitch, "for you and Milligan Creek. But we're confident that with a little fortitude—the old-fashioned kind, not the big green monstrosity version—we can turn this ship around."

Dean made a sound like a foghorn and pretended to pull an imaginary cord above his head as he held a ship's steering wheel.

"That'll be enough, Dean," Matt said, having barely tolerated his first outburst. Dean pouted but said nothing.

The mayor took a moment to digest everything the boys had just presented to him, then sat back in his chair. "I appreciate your enthusiasm, boys, and your support, but like you said, my approval rating is in the toilet. Let's face it, I'm yesterday's news. Young pups like Theo are the future of this town, not old dogs like me."

"That's exactly the problem," Matt said. "If you close your eyes and think of the future, what do you see?"

The boys all stared expectantly at Mayor Bondar, who took a moment to clue in. "Oh, you mean you want me to actually do that? Close my eyes? Right now?" The boys nodded vigorously. Mayor Bondar closed his eyes and pressed his lips together. "Well, when I think of the future, I see—"

"Does it look anything like a short guy with slicked-back hair, glasses, and a bow tie?" Matt asked.

"No, what I see is—"

"Exactly," Matt said. "Sure, people like Theo Hicken-looper might think they represent the future, but open your eyes, and you'll see the future standing right in front of you."

Mayor Bondar opened his eyes and looked around. "Where? Where's the future?"

"Right here!" Matt said, pointing to himself and the other boys. "We're the future, and even though we're too young to vote, we want a say in the direction this town takes, for better or for worse. And with you at the helm, sir, things can only get better."

"But according to Comptroller Radom, I'm the one who got the town into this mess."

"Which is why you're the only one who can get us out of it," Matt said, pointing his finger at the mayor to emphasize his point.

Mayor Bondar sat back in his chair and frowned, steepling his fingers as he pondered Matt's words. "I'm not sure I understand how those two points are—"

"As Matt noted before, sir, the details aren't important," Andrew said. "What matters is, this town needs your leadership. They just don't know it yet. We'd like to help change that—if you'll give us a chance."

Mayor Bonder spun slowly back and forth in his chair, his fingertips pressed together and his lips pursed as he squinted at the boys' eager faces. Finally, he took a deep breath and puffed out his cheeks as he exhaled. "Ah, what the heck, it's not like things could get any worse."

"You won't regret this, sir," Matt said, stepping forward and shaking the mayor's hand. "By the time we're finished, Theo Hickenlooper won't know what hit him."

12

No Such Thing as a Bad Idea

"The first thing we've got to come up with is a slogan," Matt said the following afternoon as he paced back and forth in their tree house, one hand on his chin, the other supporting his elbow. They had convinced the mayor to meet there, arguing that a new setting would inspire fresh ideas. Matt paused in front of a window and clenched his fists in front of his chest, his eyes widening with enthusiasm. "It's gotta be something catchy, memorable, something that'll appeal to people of all ages."

The other boys and Mayor Bondar were seated around the table inside the helicopter fuselage. Chad and Andrew were deep in thought, though Mayor Bondar couldn't seem to stay focused, too distracted by the tree house itself. "This place is remarkable," he said. "I'm glad you convinced me to come up here, though I'm a bit too old for tree houses, and I've never been much for heights. You're sure it's safe?"

"Of course," Matt replied. "We'd never do anything to jeopardize the life of our star candidate."

To Bondar's left, Dean also seemed a bit antsy, as if he was dying to share something with the others. Finally, he could contain himself no longer. "Actually, seeing as the grain terminal is at the heart of this election, last night I took the liberty of coming up with a series of campaign slogans, each one inspired by a different crop." Ever since Matt's "wild card" comment, Dean's brain had been working overtime trying to come up with ways he could prove his value to the team. This was one of his strategies for seizing the initiative.

Matt grimaced, but Mayor Bondar's face lit up. "That's a clever thought, son. Care to share some of your ideas?"

"I thought you'd never ask." Dean stood up and pulled a set of oversized cue cards out of his backpack. "These are just rough ideas, but once I got started, I couldn't stop. I think these would work great as posters, buttons, stickers, T-shirts, heck, maybe even radio and TV commercials."

"Just get to the idea," Matt said, taking a seat as he waited impatiently for Dean to begin.

Dean was about to reveal the first card, but then he hesitated and held it against his chest, blushing slightly. "Whew, now that I'm about to do this, I'm a little nervous. Promise you won't laugh?"

"Of course we won't laugh," Mayor Bondar said. "There are no bad ideas at this point. We're just spitballing here, so go for it."

Dean took a deep breath. "Alright, here we go. Well, seeing as wheat is the top crop grown around here, I thought I'd start with that." He turned the cue card around, revealing the slogan, "Wheat's up? Not your taxes! Vote Bondar."

The disclosure was met by stunned silence.

"That's it?" Matt said. "That's your big idea?"

"Well, it's only one of them," Dean replied, shuffling through his cards. "Here's another one." He turned it around, revealing the following slogan: "I 'canola' hope I have your vote!" It was accompanied by a crudely drawn image of the mayor's smiling face as he offered a thumbs-up. Dean smiled, expecting to be met by laughter, but all he got was more stunned silence. Even Mayor Bondar looked like he was beginning to regret his "no bad ideas" comment.

"Wait a second, wait a second," Dean said, sensing he was losing his audience. "You're gonna love this one." He revealed another cue card, which said, "Milligan Creek was 'barley' breathing before Bondar came along!"

"I really like this one," Dean said, pointing at each word. "Not just the play on 'barley' and 'barely' but also the nice alliteration it forms with breathing, before, Bondar . . ." His voice trailed off as he saw the glazed look in their eyes. "Aw, forget it." He tossed the rest of his cue cards on the table and slumped back down in his seat. "You guys never like my ideas."

"That's not true," Mayor Bondar said, leaning across the table and gathering the cue cards, so he could flip through them. "Is it, boys? See this one?" He held it up so he could read it. "What does it say . . . 'Get your 'flax' straight—vote Bondar.' Pretty clever, right guys?" Getting no takers, he flipped through a few more. "How about this one: 'Bondar will get this town's 'pulse' racing!'" He paused and thought for a moment. "Oh, I get it! Beans, chickpeas, lentils, peas, those are all pulse crops, right?" Dean nodded slowly, still scowling. "A bit of a stretch but still clever," Bondar said, flipping to the next one. "Let's see here, 'Want to move your oats? Give me your votes!' Or how about this one: 'How is victory 'spelt'? B-O-N-D-A-R.' Now that's a winner right there. Wow, nice work, Dean."

Dean's face brightened. "Really? You think so?"

Mayor Bondar was about to reply, but before he could, Matt cleared his throat loudly. All eyes shifted to him. "With all due respect, Mr. Mayor, Dean, these ideas are terrible."

"Well, it's not like you guys are coming up with any-thing better!" Dean said, standing up and gathering his cue cards. "If you don't like my ideas, I can just—"

"Wait a second," Andrew said, reaching for the cue cards. "May I?" he asked when Dean failed to release them. Finally, Dean let go and fell back into his seat. Everyone watched Andrew as he flipped through the cards, his brow furrowed in thought. "While I'm not a huge fan of any of these slogans . . ." He glanced up. "No offense, Dean."

"None taken," Dean said sarcastically.

"I do think Dean's on the right track."

Dean's eyes lit up. "You do?"

Suddenly, Matt pounded the table. "That's it!"

"What's it?" Mayor Bondar asked, gripping the table and looking around nervously as the tree house shud-dered slightly.

"Grain elevators, where are they located?" Matt asked.

Bondar's mind raced to catch up. "At the . . . at the north end of Main Street?"

"No! Not our grain elevators, any grain elevators." He stared at the others with wide eyes. Clearly, none of them saw the connection. "Don't you guys get it? Along the rail-way tracks. So, get this: Vote for Bondar—he'll get us back on track. Hey? What do you think?"

The others were silent for a moment. "I like the way you rhymed 'back' and 'track,'" Mayor Bondar said.

"That's it?" Matt asked in disbelief. "What about the rest of you?"

Chad shrugged. "It's okay, I guess. But if we don't get it, I guarantee no one else will make the connection."

Dean nudged Matt. "See? It's a lot harder than you think." Matt glared at him.

"If you guys would let me finish . . ." Andrew waited until everyone's attention was back on him. "Dean's slogans sparked an idea. It's simple, it cuts straight to the point, and I think you're going to love it."

Matt crossed his arms in annoyance. "Oh yeah? What makes you think that?"

In response, Andrew grabbed a sharpie out of an old soup can at the center of the table that was stuffed with writing implements and scrawled something on the back of one of Dean's cue cards. When he held it up for the others to see, he was met by a chorus of enthusiasm.

"That's brilliant!" Matt said, leaping to his feet.

"By golly, you're right," Mayor Bondar agreed.

"Let's not forget Dean," Chad said, noting his friend sulking in his chair. "If he hadn't been brave enough to get the ball rolling, we never would have gotten here." He winked at Dean, who couldn't help but smile.

"Thanks, Chad."

"Well, what do we do now?" Mayor Bondar asked, rubbing his hands together. "I can't wait to get started."

"Leave that to us," Matt said, already on his feet. "Come on, boys, we've got a campaign to run."

13

POUNDING THE PAVEMENT

The following Saturday morning, Tom Pew, a spindly old bachelor with grizzled whiskers sprouting from his sun-wrinkled face, pushed up the back of his tweed newsboy hat and scratched his head as he read Mayor Bondar's campaign poster. It was pinned to the bulletin board outside the co-op store on Main Street. "'Elevate your vote,' he says. 'Don't let Hickenlooper make Milligan Creek a terminal case.' What the heck is that supposed to mean?"

He turned to Howard Long, his best friend and verbal sparring partner since high school. Both men had long since retired from farming and moved to town. Now they spent most of their days bickering on the bench outside the co-op. When it got too cold or rainy to be outside, they swapped tales, drank coffee, and flirted with the widows at the seniors' center down the street.

"It means the same thing every politician has ever said since time began," Howard replied. "Bondar wants to fill his pockets—with our money!"

The crusty old-timers shared a laugh as they sat down on the bench and resumed their perusal of the traffic, waving at people they knew and casting a suspicious glare at anyone who even remotely looked like they were from out of town.

"Not quite the reaction I was hoping for," Andrew said as he and the other boys finished taping another poster around a lamppost on the corner, having overheard the conversation.

"Ah, forget those geezers," Chad said. "They hate everybody. I think it's a great slogan that cuts right to the point, way better than anything Dean or Matt came up with. Speaking of which, I wonder how their door-to-door canvassing is going."

§

Dean and Matt walked down one of Milligan Creeks numerous tree-lined streets, both of them dressed in a blazer, shirt, and tie. For once, Matt had left his trademark Edmonton Oilers cap at home. The boys' hair was carefully styled too, though Matt's required less work, seeing as he had shaved his head earlier that summer and was still in the process of growing it back.

Dean tugged at his shirt collar and swallowed hard. "Were the suits and ties really necessary? My mom bought me this thing for my cousin's wedding three years ago, and I've grown at least three inches since then. I mean, look at the sleeves." He held up his hand, and his suit jacket sleeve slid halfway up his forearm. "I look like Boris Karloff's Frankenstein in this thing." Dean was just getting into classic monster films, which had begun airing every weekend at midnight on channel six, hence the obscure movie reference.

"Well, just pull it down," Matt said, adjusting it for

him. "And don't raise your arm like that. We need to look respectable." He paused in front of a short cement sidewalk that led to a small, cozy-looking single-story house. "Alright, your turn."

Dean sighed as he pulled out a campaign poster. "What do I say again?"

"Just smile, introduce yourself, hand the person a poster, invite them to the mayoral debate, and ask them if Mayor Bondar can count on their vote."

"What if they're not home?"

"Just stick the flyer between the screen door and their main door. And hurry up about it. We have a lot of ground to cover today."

Dean sighed again, then trudged up the sidewalk and rang the doorbell. As soon as he did, a small dog started barking inside. Dean waited about five seconds and then put his hand on the screen door. "Looks like nobody's home." He was about to open it and slip in a flyer when the inside door flew open, revealing Darcy, the teenage delivery van driver for the Milligan Creek Co-op. In his arms was a small fluffy white dog. The minute she saw Dean, she started snarling and snapping.

"Mindy, stop it!" Darcy said, putting his hand around her snout and clamping it shut. She continued to whine and growl as he turned back to Dean, speaking to him through the screen door. "What do you want?"

Dean's face flushed. Earlier that summer, he had accidentally vomited all over Darcy after stowing away inside the co-op's delivery van en route to assassinating his target during the water war. He hadn't seen Darcy face to face since then, having gone out of his way to avoid him for fear of retribution.

"Well?" Darcy said. "I haven't got all day."

Dean heard the TV playing a football game in the background. Keeping his eyes on his spit-shined shoes, which he had stayed up late polishing the night before, he held out the campaign poster, hoping his slicked-back hair, his suit, and the screen door would be enough to mask his identity. After all, he had been wearing a hoodie on the day of the vomiting incident, and it had all happened so fast. "Can we count on your vote for Mayor Bondar in this fall's election?"

Darcy pushed the screen door open far enough to snatch the flyer out of Dean's hand. He looked at it. "Mayor Bondar? Old cue ball? I've got peaches in my fridge with more hair on them than that old coot. Why the heck would I vote for him?"

"Well, uh, he's, uh . . ." Dean glanced at Matt for moral support and then turned back to Darcy. "A vote for Mayor Bondar is a vote to keep Milligan Creek on the map."

Darcy raised one eyebrow and stared at him in confusion. "Huh?"

"You know, Theo Hickenlooper, the other candidate, he wants Fortitude to tear down the grain elevators at the north end of Main Street and build a big ugly inland terminal on the edge of town."

"So? What do I care about some stupid old grain elevators?"

"Uh . . ."

"Besides, I'm not even old enough to vote."

Dean looked at him in surprise. For the past couple of years, Darcy had been capable of growing a full beard, which he did every spring during NHL hockey playoffs, often wearing it right through the summer. "You aren't? Well, uh, are your parents home then?"

"No, they're not, and—" Darcy paused and squinted.

"Hey, wait a second, don't I know you?" He pushed the screen door open, his eyes lighting up with recognition. "Yeah, you're that kid! The one who—"

"Gotta go!" Dean leaped off the front step and ran across Darcy's lawn. Matt gaped at him, having not heard the exchange. "Dean! Where are you going?"

On the doorstep, Darcy un-clamped his hand from Mindy's snout and set her down. The minute her scrabbling paws made contact with the ground, she took off after Dean, snapping and snarling. "Get 'im, Mindy! Run!"

"Help!" Dean cried as he raced down the street, the little puffball hot on his heels and a handful of campaign flyers spiraling to the ground in his wake.

"Hey, wait up!" Matt cried, scooping up flyers and snatching them out of the air as he ran after Dean.

"And tell old cue ball to take his vote and—" Before Darcy ended his sentence, Matt had rounded the corner and was out of earshot.

§

Several hours later, all four boys convened at Dean's house, sitting around his kitchen table eating gingersnaps and drinking lemonade. They were hot and tired, having tramped all over town putting up posters and canvassing door to door in the unseasonably warm fall weather. Dean had taken off his blazer, loosened his tie, and rolled up his sleeves. He looked like a junior executive after a hard day, and it had been a hard day.

Following the Mindy incident, Dean and Matt had several other stressful encounters. Thankfully, none of them entailed the need to run for their lives. However, one old woman mistook the two well-dressed young men for missionaries going door-to-door. No matter how many times the boys tried to convince her otherwise, she insisted on sitting them down and giving them her take on how the universe was created and where humans came from.

"I think she's been watching too many of the same late-night movies as Dean," Matt said. "With all that talk about UFOs and aliens, I was starting to think *she* was an alien, and she was just delaying us until her mother ship showed up to take us away."

"Who's an alien?" Mrs. Muller asked, breezing through the front door laden with bags of groceries, which she plunked down on the table, sending plates, plastic glasses, and cookies flying. "And how much do we have to pay them to take Matt away and never bring him back?"

"Very funny, Mom," Dean said, wiping lemonade off the front of his shirt. "And can you be a little more careful? You're the one who's always complaining about how much laundry you have to do."

Mrs. Muller paused to catch her breath, eyeing the well-dressed boys suspiciously. "Where did you all just come from, a funeral?" Suddenly, she spotted a stack of campaign posters on the table, the top copy of which was spattered with lemonade, which Matt was wiping off with his necktie. "Did Bondar's goons come by today trying to get my vote?" She swiped the poster out of Matt's hand and read it out loud. "Elevate your vote? Don't let Hickenlooper make Milligan Creek a terminal case? Hmph. I bet whoever came up with that slogan thought he was pretty clever."

Matt, Chad, and Dean all glanced at Andrew, who had his eyes fixed on the table's Formica surface, his cheeks glowing slightly.

"I'm sure they had plenty of other good ideas," Dean said, giving the other boys a meaningful look. He was still smarting from their rejection of his grain-themed slogans.

"And why did they leave so many flyers here?" Mrs. Muller asked, zipping through the stack with her thumb like a Vegas dealer shuffling a deck of cards. "Do they think I'm going to do their dirty work for them, hand these out to my friends and family?"

"Actually," Matt said, "we're Bondar's 'goons,' and we're the ones handing them out. On that note, can Mayor Bondar count on your vote?"

Mrs. Muller gawked at Matt in astonishment. Then she stepped forward and put her thumb and forefinger above and below his eye and forced it open as she stared into it.

"What the heck are you doing?" Dean asked.

"Yeah, what are you doing?" Matt said, pulling away.

"Just checking," Mrs. Muller said, scooping up a bag of frozen goods and heading for the basement stairs.

"For what?" Dean asked.

"To see if that old lady didn't replace Matt with a cleverly disguised alien replacement." With that, she retreated downstairs, where their deep freeze was located

The boys all looked at each other and then broke out laughing. Even Matt had to chuckle, considering their "close encounter" earlier that day. Then his face grew serious. He took a deep breath and let it out slowly as he held up one of the posters and looked at it. "I don't know, guys, maybe we are wasting our time."

"What do you mean?" Chad asked.

Matt spun the poster onto the table. "Think about all the rejection we faced today. And if we can't even convince our own parents to vote for Bondar, what hope do we have of persuading people we don't even know?"

"Well, to be fair, my mom is pretty much guaranteed to reject anything you're in favor of," Dean pointed out. "And seeing as my family is the only one who lives in town, technically, my mom and dad are the only ones among our parents who can vote."

Matt sighed again. "I guess. But it's the principle of the thing. It just feels like everyone's convinced that Bondar's time is done."

"I wouldn't give up just yet," Andrew said. "We hit practically the entire town today, and many of those people weren't home. I think we have to wait a bit to see how effective our efforts have been. The debate's coming up soon, and that could change everything."

14

A BAD RAP

Theo grinned as he sat behind his desk reading the latest issue of the *Milligan Creek Review*, which featured his face above the fold on page two. It was part of a series of profiles that the paper was doing on the mayoral and town council candidates leading up to the election, which was just two weeks away.

"I'm glad I spent the extra money on those professional headshots," he said to Rudy Bricksaw, who was sitting in a chair across from him. After resigning as Bondar's campaign manager, Rudy had quickly defected to Theo's team. A small man, Rudy had managed to survive in life by attaching himself to winners, a strategy he first employed back in high school, when some older students bullied him.

"They make Bondar look like the rank amateur that he is," Theo continued, snatching the previous week's paper off his desk and opening it to compare the photos. Unlike Theo's photo, which was well lit and obviously taken in a studio, Bondar's photo was blown out and slightly blurred, like someone had taken it on a cheap camera while riding past Bondar on a ten-speed bike. "I've seen photos of the

Loch Ness Monster that are clearer than that."

Rudy leaned forward and nodded slightly as he looked at the photos, though Theo's smile failed to ignite a similar expression on the shoe salesman's face. Instead, Rudy's lips were pursed and his eyebrows bunched together in a frown, the same expression he got every time he had to deliver bad news to a superior.

Finally, Theo tore his eyes away from the photos and leaned back in his chair, looking at his campaign manager for the first time. "So tell me, how are the poll numbers? Is anyone planning to vote for Bondar, least of all admit it?"

"Well, that's why I wanted to talk to you this morning. I—"

Before Rudy could finish, Theo snatched the paper Rudy was holding out of his hand. His eyes narrowed as he scanned the numbers. "You've got to be kidding me. He *gained* two points? How is that possible?"

"Well, part of it may be due to this," Rudy said, sliding a copy of Bondar's campaign poster across Theo's desk. Theo scrutinized it as Rudy continued. "His youthful campaign team has been papering the town with them. Not only that, over the weekend they went to every house in the community on Bondar's behalf, I even heard that—"

"Spare me the details," Theo said, dropping the poster onto his desk. "Youthful campaign team? Who are these guys? And why are they working for him, not me?"

"I don't know, Theo, I—"

"I thought I told you to keep a close eye on Bondar."

"You did, but that was a lot easier when I was managing his campaign."

"Well, how can you manage my campaign if you're managing his campaign?"

106

"That's exactly my point, Theo. There's only so much I can—"

"More importantly, why are these young people supporting Bondar?" He pulled a mirror out of his drawer, which he used periodically throughout the day to check his hair, and inspected his reflection, making sure he had nothing stuck between his straight white teeth. "I'm the face of the future in this community, not that old fart. Why are they supporting him?"

"It could have something to do with the grain elevators, sir."

Theo lowered the mirror and looked at Rudy. "The grain elevators? What do you mean?"

"It's right there on the poster," Rudy said, thumping it with his forefinger. "Elevate your vote. Don't make Milligan Creek a terminal case."

"I can read," Theo said. "My point is, why do these kids care if we get rid of some old grain elevators? Kids are supposed to care about the future, not the past."

Rudy shrugged. "Maybe these kids are different."

Theo leaned back in his chair and pondered the situation as he stared at the ceiling. "Does the high school still run an archery program, Rudy?"

"I don't know. It's been a few years since my kids—"

"Then find out," Theo said, standing up. "And find out who's in it. And while you're at it, find out everything you can about Bondar's campaign team. I want names, photos, birth dates, any dirt you can dig up on them."

"Where are you going?" Rudy asked as Theo headed for the door. "I thought we were going to go over the material for next week's debate."

"The debate can wait," Theo replied, throwing on his coat. "First, I need to pick up a bit of insurance."

"But you're an insurance salesman," Rudy said, standing up. "Why are you—"

"Just do your job, Rudy, and I'll do mine."

§

"My name is Michael, and I'm your mayor. With Theo at the helm, this town ain't got a prayer. Bald I may be-uh but my head's fulla ideas. So if you don't want Milligan Creek to reek take a sneak peek at my cheat sheet, fool, and let me take you to school. Fortitude's the wrong attitude, listen dude! Hickenlooper's a blooper, even worse, a storm trooper. So if you're like me and you love grain let me make it plain, Jane, remember my name. You gotta rock to my talk and quote me by rote, Bondar's the one for your vote."

Dean looked up from the paper on which the rap he had just recited was written. "After that part, I thought the four of us could come on stage in sunglasses with our hats on sideways and stand in a circle around Mayor Bondar as we rap the chorus, 'Elevate your vote,' three times while Mayor Bondar echoes with 'Hear me now,' and then we all do a big finish with, 'Don't let what's-his-face make us a terminal case,' ending with our arms crossed and our backs to each other like this." He demonstrated by crossing his arms and leaning against the wall, his hat on sideways and wearing sunglasses, just as he described. Finally, he stood up straight and took off his sunglasses. "So, what do you think?"

His question was met by stunned silence as Mayor Bondar and the rest of the boys sat in a semicircle around him in the mayor's office.

"It's certainly . . . innovative," Mayor Bondar said.

"Rap is the hottest thing in music right now," Dean said. "Breakdancing too. In fact, while you're rapping, I've been working on learning the worm, and—"

"I hate to rain on your parade," Andrew said. "But let me remind you of Milligan Creek's demographics." He put a chart up on the bulletin board. "The median age of this town is fifty years old. That means at least half the voters likely haven't even heard of rap music."

"And those who have probably hate it," Chad pointed out.

"I certainly don't like the sound of rap music—whatever it is," Mayor Bondar said.

"Are you kidding me?" Dean asked. "I stayed up half the night writing that. Doesn't anybody else think it's a good idea?" He looked around the room. No one would even meet his gaze, much less agree with him. Finally, he sank down into his chair with a huff. "Fine. That's the last time I offer any more ideas."

"Dean, I don't mean to be discouraging, but . . ."

"I think what the mayor is trying to say is that you can't argue with the facts," Chad said, earning a nod from Bondar. "The rap would be a great idea if he were running for school president, but this is a serious election. And let's face it, Mayor Bondar's . . ."

"Old," Matt said, tired of watching Chad grimace as he struggled to come up with a non-offensive descriptor. "No offense, Mayor Bondar."

"Relatively speaking," Andrew added, trying to soften the blow.

"Yes, relative to us," Matt said, picking up the thread. "What I mean is—"

"I know what you mean," Dean said. "We're going to go with one of your ideas, not mine, like always."

"Excuse me," Mayor Bondar said, getting out of his chair. "Before we toss this idea out, let's at least give it the old college try. May I?" He held his hand out to Dean.

"Are you serious?" Dean asked.

The mayor nodded, so Dean handed him the script. "I'll take the rest of that get-up too," Bondar said, indicating Dean's cap and sunglasses.

"If you say so," Dean said, handing them to him.

Mayor Bondar put them on, turned the cap sideways, and cleared his throat, gesturing like a rapper with his free hand as he read the script. "My name is Michael, and I'm your mayor. With Theo at the helm this town ain't got a prayer . . ."

Outside the door, Rudy Bricksaw's eyes lit up as he listened to the mayor's sick beats. Rap music! So that was the secret to reaching younger voters. *Well, two can play at that game*, he thought as he hurried off, already concocting the first line of Theo's rap in his head.

Back inside the room, the boys tried to keep a straight face, but then all of them, including Dean, burst into laughter, doubling over in their chairs. Even Mayor Bondar joined in, laughing so hard that he was unable to continue.

"Okay, okay, I surrender!" Dean said. "It was a terrible idea."

"But funny," Chad said.

"Indeed it was," Mayor Bondar said, taking off the sunglasses and hat and sitting back down, a bit breathless. "In fact, if you don't mind, I'd like to keep this and rap it for my wife tonight."

"Be my guest," Dean said.

"On a more serious note," Andrew said, standing up

and pinning another piece of paper to the bulletin board, "I've made a list of the pros and cons of the grain terminal, so if you want to start memorizing these talking points for the debate . . ."

15

A Crucial Test

"And finally, controversy broke out today at a dog show in Regina when a man insisted that he be allowed to enter a unique candidate in the ugliest dog competition—himself!"

Seated behind the anchor's desk at the Channel Six News studio, Tucker grinned as the monitors showed a man whose curly white hair and beard made him look remarkably similar to a poodle with a bad case of mange.

"When asked why he wanted to do it, the man, Mr. Randall Kotter of Invermay, Saskatchewan, said his beloved seventeen-year-old Schnauzer, Nancy, died two weeks before the competition, so he wanted to take home top prize in her honor. Once organizers confirmed that nothing in the rulebook explicitly forbade humans from entering the competition—a loophole they plan to close for next year—Mr. Kotter was allowed to compete. It was a close race, but he came in second, losing to a cross-eyed, hairless Chinese Crested hound named Bruce."

The image on the monitor changed to show what was likely the ugliest dog in the world, never mind Saskatchewan, its eyes not only crossed but also different colors, a wisp of scraggly white hair protruding from its mottled black skin.

"That's it for today's newscast and my stint here behind the desk. It's been a fun week filling in for Sandy, who'll be back in the studio on Monday. That means I'll be back out among you, the people—live, loud, and on location. Goodnight!"

Tucker shuffled the papers on his desk as the newscast's closing music played. The director counted down with his fingers, going from five to one, and then made a slashing motion across his throat. "And . . . cut. Nice work, Tucker."

"Thanks, Glen," Tucker said, gathering his things. "It's been a pleasure working with you."

He was about to head to his dressing room when he heard a solitary pair of hands clapping somewhere in the darkness beyond the bright studio lights. Tucker squinted and shielded his eyes. He saw the silhouette of a short man wearing glasses and a suit. A moment later, the figure stepped into the light, still clapping.

"Hello!" Tucker said, stepping down off the riser as the director and the rest of the crew filed out of the studio. "To what do I owe the honor, Mr. . . ."

"Hickenlooper," Theo said, extending his hand as he approached. "Theo Hickenlooper. We met the other day when you covered the arrow incident in Milligan Creek."

Tucker's eyes lit up as he shook Theo's hand. "Of course! Nice to see you again. Have the police found the culprit yet?"

"No, but they're sparing no effort in their search, and I have every confidence they'll find the perpetrator soon."

"Good to hear. The RCMP detachment in that town is top notch. What's the name of the staff sergeant again? Romanchuk?"

"Romanowski."

"Right. Nice fellow. Amazing mustache. I met him while covering that radio show thing down at the duck marsh earlier this spring. They ever find out who did that?"

"Not as far as I know," Theo said.

There was an awkward pause as the two men stared at each other.

"So," Tucker began, "what can I—" He stopped when Theo pulled out a copy of Tucker's autobiography. "Ah, my book! You want an autograph." He felt his jacket pockets for a pen, then shifted to his pants. "Doesn't look like I have a pen on me, but maybe Lucy . . ." He looked around for his producer. "Where has that woman gone off to anyway?"

"Got you covered," Theo said, producing a sharpie. "Speaking of 'covered,' that photo of you on the back cover is fantastic. I should get the contact information for your photographer."

"Oh?" Tucker said as he scrawled his signature. "Thinking of writing your own book?"

"Possibly. After I win the election, that is."

Tucker glanced up at him. "Election?"

Theo held out a campaign button. It said, "Vote for Hickenlooper, He's Super!" over a photo of his smiling face. It was a strangely disturbing image. "Yes. I'm running for mayor of Milligan Creek. Here, take it, I have plenty."

Tucker returned the book to Theo, then held his hands in front of his chest, palms out, as he took a step back. "I'm sorry, but I can't accept gifts from candidates, no matter how small—the gift, that is, not the candidate," he added, noting Theo's pint-size stature. "Wouldn't want to compromise my journalistic integrity. Have to remain objective and all that."

115

"Of course, of course," Theo said, pocketing the button. He glanced around the empty studio. "So, you've been here, what, three years now?"

"Yep." Tucker took a deep breath of the musty studio air. The roof had a leak that the maintenance crew was still trying to locate, but Tucker had been working there for so long that he didn't even smell it anymore. "Three of the best years of my life."

"It's a shame, really," Theo said.

Tucker frowned. "Excuse me?"

"You know, a man of your talents, stuck in a place like . . . this." He held up his arms to indicate the studio, which was quite dumpy now that Tucker thought about it.

"This place isn't so bad," Tucker said. "Besides, I don't plan to stay a reporter forever. In fact, the way things have been going lately, I feel like it's only a matter of time before they bump me up to weekend anchor."

Theo smiled, an unnerving gesture. "Weekend anchor? Really? I thought a man like you would have his sights set on . . . bigger things."

"I do!" Tucker replied. "In fact, if you read step seven in my book . . ." His voice trailed off as Theo turned his back to Tucker and strode up to the riser. "Uh, you really shouldn't go up there, Mr. Hickenlooper, unless you're a . . ."

Ignoring Tucker, Theo ran his hand along the anchor desk, then turned to face the cameras, which were dark and silent. "I can see it now," he said, spreading his hands in a dramatic gesture as he broke into the intro song for the CBC's ten o'clock news broadcast. "Ba-da-ba-ba-ba-da-ba-da, ba-da-ba-ba-ba-ba-da-ba-da . . . the National, with Tucker Butker."

Tucker smiled. "I like the sound of that."

"And so you should. You were meant to captain that

116

ship, Tucker. It's your destiny."

"It is? I mean, yes, it is!" Tucker's entire body swelled with elation as he closed his eyes and pictured himself anchoring the top national news broadest in the country. The fame, the money, the free meals in every restaurant in town . . . Then the musty air in his lungs brought his mind crashing back down to reality. He opened his eyes and frowned. "Wait a second, what does that have to do with you?"

Theo stepped down off the riser and approached Tucker. "People like you and me, we can't just sit around and wait for Lady Luck to smile on us, can we? We have to create our own luck."

"Yes, in fact—"

"The way I see it, you want to get somewhere, and so do I. So, perhaps there's a way that we can help each other. That is what lesson nine in your book is all about, isn't it? 'A fast current moves all the canoes'?"

"Yes, but you're a politician, and I'm a—" Suddenly, Tucker's eyes widened with understanding. "Oh, I get it! This is a test! You're testing me, to see how honest I am. Is this part of a job interview? Was I not just filling in for Sandy? Was that some kind of an audition? If so, did I get the job? Is someone filming this somewhere?" He shielded his eyes from the studio lights and peered into the darkness. "Lucy? Bill? Are you out there? If so, the jig is up. I'm on to you!"

"Nobody's out there, Tucker," Theo said, stepping closer. "And no, this is not a test—at least not the kind you're thinking of. All I'm saying is, if we get our paddles in rhythm, who knows? Maybe we can row, row, row our boat all the way to the top. I'm not asking you to do anything right now except think about it."

He pulled out his campaign button and set it on the

117

anchor desk and then began singing the theme song from *The National* as he pretended to paddle his way out of the studio. "Ba-da-ba-ba-ba-ba-da-ba-da . . ."

Before Tucker knew it, Theo was gone, leaving him to wonder if he had dreamed the entire scenario. But there it was on the desk, the campaign button, proof that Theo and his offer were all too real.

"It might have worked too," Tucker said. "But Mr. Hickenlooper forgot three things. One, you don't row a canoe, you paddle it. Two, water flows downhill, so there's no way we can paddle our way to the top. And three, I'm Tucker Butker, and this is one reporter who's going to keep his integrity intact!"

With that, he flicked the campaign button, sending it skittering across the desk and into the garbage can, where it rattled around in a circle before finally settling into place. A moment later, the soundproof studio door whooshed shut as Tucker left.

In the silence that followed, the scraping of a high-heeled shoe resounded from the back of the room, followed by a clopping sound as a woman walked down from the top of the stadium seating and approached the riser. A hand reached into the garbage can and pulled out the campaign button. The hand belonged to none other than Lucy Barnes, Tucker's producer. As she ran her thumb over the button's smooth laminated surface, she smiled, the expression looking no more natural for her than it did for Theo. "Tucker may not appreciate the value of your offer, Mr. Hickenlooper," she said, "but leave that little detail to me."

The studio echoed with the clicking of her high heels as she walked out, followed by the whoosh of the door.

Seconds later, the door to the equipment room squeaked open, and Bill, the cameraman, peeked out.

16

BRAINSTORMING

"Just to give you a general overview, boys, there are two basic ways that municipalities can improve their bottom line." Mayor Bondar scribbled two terms at the top of the whiteboard and then underlined each and drew a long vertical line between them, forming two columns. The group had gathered in the mayor's office to come up with new ideas to share at the all-candidates' debate, which was only a couple of days away. "Cutting costs and raising revenues."

Dean leaned over to Matt, all four boys sitting on chairs arranged in a semicircle around Mayor Bondar. "For an adult, he sure has messy writing," Dean whispered. Matt shushed him with an elbow to the ribs.

Mayor Bondar stood back and looked at the whiteboard, then turned to the boys. "So, I suggest we focus our brainstorming on these two areas while preparing for the debate. Any ideas?" He looked at them expectantly, whiteboard marker at the ready.

"Can you give us an example of each to get us started?" Andrew asked.

Mayor Bondar took a deep breath through his nose

before replying. He loved the smell of whiteboard markers, which was one reason why he loved brainstorming sessions. He was convinced the smell stimulated his imagination. "Raising property taxes is one of the simplest and most obvious ways to increase revenues," he said, writing it on the board, though to the boys it looked like he had written "pronty toxes."

"As for cutting costs," the mayor continued, moving over to the next column, "one of the biggest budget items for any municipality is staff salaries, so we could look at cutting those or possibly even reducing the size of our staff or the number of hours they work each week." He made note of that on the whiteboard as well, though it was equally illegible, then turned to face the boys. "Though I have to admit, neither of those options are going to create a stampede to the polling booth on my behalf, so it would be better if we came up with some more creative ideas that are relatively painless for the average voter."

The boys were all silent for a moment, their brains churning.

"How about user fees?" Chad asked. "You know, admission to the pool, the skating rink, things like that. Could we raise those?"

Mayor Bondar winced. "Once again, that's going to hit people right in the pocketbook, and it's going to hit families with young kids the hardest. Not exactly the best way to win hearts and minds."

"What about licenses?" Andrew said. "Business licenses, pet licenses, that sort of thing."

"We could look at that," Mayor Bondar said, writing it on the board. "We haven't raised those fees in quite some time."

"You need a license to own a pet?" Dean asked. "Do

you need to take an owner's exam too?"

"Generally, just dogs require a license," Mayor Bondar said. "And no, there's no exam," he added with a grin. "Not for the owner or the dog."

"That hardly seems fair," Matt said. "Why are dog owners the only ones penalized?"

Mayor Bondar paused to think about it. "You know, I've never thought to ask that question before."

"Probably because dogs are the ones who do their business on other people's property, and their owners never clean up after them," Dean said. His mother had forced him to pick up more than his fair share of doggy doo from his family's front yard, left there by careless neighbors.

"Yeah, but cats can be a menace too," Matt argued. "Think about how bad your sandbox used to stink, Dean. Your parents eventually had to get rid of it. Turtles can also be a hazard. Remember what Henrietta told us about people setting their turtles free in wetlands areas, totally disrupting the local ecosystem?" Henrietta Blunt was the director of the Milligan Creek Heritage Marsh, which was located just fifteen minutes north of town. The boys had gone on a field trip to the marsh earlier that year. "How about a license on turtles?"

"Well, I hardly think—"

"And why draw the line there?" Matt continued before the mayor could finish. "How about snakes? Gerbils? Guinea pigs? Goldfish? Rats? Pot-bellied pigs? They could all be let into the wild too, creating all sorts of problems. Ever heard about the alligators in New York's sewers?"

"I appreciate your thinking," Mayor Bondar said, trying his best to sound conciliatory, "but the number of people who own such pets in town is likely quite small, so even if we did impose such licenses, it would be a drop in the bucket. Not to mention it would make us look quite petulant, if you'll pardon the turn of phrase."

"Pet you what?" Dean asked.

"Speaking of pets," Chad said, ignoring Dean's question, "what do people in town do when a pet dies?"

"Well, I suppose they mourn it for a while," Mayor Bondar said, "and then they probably get a new one."

"No, I mean—yes, of course they do," Chad said, "but what do they do with the body?"

Mayor Bondar shrugged. "I assume they bury it."

Chad jabbed his index finger in the mayor's direction. "Exactly. But where? Isn't there a bylaw against burying pets in your backyard?"

"Yes, I suppose there is," Mayor Bondar replied.

"Then let's make it easier for people and create a pet cemetery," Chad said. "A special graveyard just for pets."

"That's a great idea!" Matt exclaimed. "The town can sell burial plots, mini gravestones, even little pet coffins. We could even get some of the local ministers on board to hold pet funerals!"

"Now you're talking!" Mayor Bondar said, writing the idea on the board.

"In fact, we could even use the land where Fortitude wants to build the inland terminal," Chad added.

"Great idea!" Mayor Bondar said as he finished scribbling. Thankfully, Andrew was also taking notes on a clipboard. His handwriting was much neater than the mayor's.

"Um, aren't you guys forgetting something?" Dean asked.

Everyone looked at him. "What?" Matt said.

"Pet Sematary, the Stephen King novel? Do you want this entire town overrun with zombie cats, dogs, and goldfish?"

The other boys rolled their eyes and then redirected their attention back to the whiteboard. "You really need to upgrade your reading material," Matt said.

Andrew looked up from his clipboard. "You know, I was just thinking about the Trans Canada Trail."

"What about it?" Mayor Bondar asked.

"My grandma bought me a section of it for my birthday—that is, she paid for a section of the trail in my name, so my name is somewhere along the trail on a plaque. What if we did the same thing for the storm sewers that need replacing? We could get people or businesses to sponsor a segment and then put plaques along the street indicating who paid for what part."

"I can see it now," Matt said, waving his arms dramatically as if he was pitching a scene from a movie. "Feeling 'flushed,' like your life has gone down the toilet? Have we got a deal for you!"

Chad and Dean chuckled, but Andrew's face reddened slightly, partly out of embarrassment and partly from anger. "Storm sewers are for carrying rainfall runoff and other drainage," he said, "not sewage."

"Oh," Matt said. "Really?"

"That's a great idea, Andrew," Mayor Bondar said, "but like Matt said, the moment most people hear the word 'sewer,' their mind will go straight into the gutter, so to speak." He paused to grin at his own joke. "But that actually sparked another good idea—advertising. As you were talking, I was thinking about all the buildings and vehicles the town owns. What if we sold advertising space on them to local businesses?"

"That's brilliant," Matt said as the mayor wrote it on the board.

The group continued to brainstorm ideas throughout

123

the afternoon, considering all sorts of schemes, from installing parking meters on Main Street to converting the splash park into a coin-operated system, increasing late fees on library books, charging people by the pound for the amount of garbage they produced each week, and reducing the number of times town workers cut the grass and performed other services in Milligan Creek's parks and public spaces.

"What about cutting salaries?" Andrew said during a lull in the conversation. "I realize you said that idea wouldn't be very popular, but what about cutting one salary in particular."

"Which one might that be?" Mayor Bondar asked.

"Yours."

The mayor's eyebrows shot up. "Mine? But—"

"Think about what a powerful symbolic gesture that would be," Andrew said. "How much do you make each year as mayor?"

"Well, I hardly think it's appropriate to ask such—"

"Isn't it recorded in the town council's minutes?" Andrew said. "We could simply look it up."

Mayor Bondar sighed. "Yes, it is. I make ten thousand dollars a year. It's hardly a fortune."

"Exactly," Andrew said. "I'm sure you could live without it. At least for the short term."

"But what about—"

"You're a retired teacher, aren't you?"

"Yes, but—"

"So you probably get a good pension from that, right?"

"Yes," Mayor Bondar admitted. "But still—"

"And your wife operates her own store." She ran Milligan Creek's only florist shop, which did good business considering it was the only one for miles around.

The mayor sighed. "Yes."

"So, think about how impressed people would be if for the first year of your next term you donated your salary back to the town to help cover some of these costs. You could even challenge people to match your donation. What's that come to, about eight dollars and fifty cents per person? That's twenty thousand dollars in revenue right there, and people would hardly feel the pinch."

"I would," Mayor Bondar said, his dreams of a two-week holiday in Cuba evaporating before his eyes. "But I take your point." He wrote it at the bottom of the "Cutting Costs" column, which was already crammed with ideas. He turned back to the group with a forlorn look on his face. "Any other 'brilliant' ideas? I could always sell my house or my car, and my wife and I could live in a tent for the first year of my next term."

"Would you?" Matt asked, his face brightening at the thought. "That's a great idea. We could even sell advertising on the tent. Heck, maybe a TV station would even be willing to embed a cameraman with you guys and make a show out of it. Think of how much money that would generate. We already know Tucker Butker, and he could—"

"There is no way I'm spending a year in a tent with or without Tucker Butker," Mayor Bondar said. "I was merely joking." He put the cap on his whiteboard marker and stretched. "I think we have more than enough good ideas for now. Let's convene tomorrow after we've all had a chance to process."

Outside the door to the mayor's office, Rudy Bricksaw finished making a few notes of his own, then slipped out before anyone saw him.

17

AN UNSETTLING ENCOUNTER

Following the brainstorming session at the mayor's office, Dean was riding his bike home when he came across a white Honda Civic parked on the side of the street. That was nothing unusual, but the man crouched by the left-rear wheel certainly was. It was none other than Theo, and he appeared to be repairing a flat tire.

When Theo heard Dean approaching, he stood up and wiped his forehead with his arm. The sleeves of his white dress shirt were rolled up, and his blazer was hanging from the driver's side mirror. Dean slowed as he drew close to the car.

"Hello!" Theo said in an overly friendly voice.

"Hello," Dean said uncertainly as he rolled to a stop.

"Theo Hickenlooper, mayoral candidate in this fall's election." Theo stepped forward and offered his uncharacteristically greasy hand to Dean, who shook it warily.

"Yes, I recognize you."

"Wouldn't you know it? Another flat tire," Theo said. "First the arrow, and now this." He held up a rusty nail that, apparently, he had extracted from the flat. "You'd think someone was out to get me."

Dean's cheeks flared slightly. Theo's comment was a bit too close for comfort. "Well, accidents happen. Do you want me to call a tow truck or something? I only live a block away."

"No, that won't be necessary," Theo said. "I managed to get the spare on myself."

"Okay then," Dean said, starting to pull away. "Sorry about your luck."

"So, you only live a block away from here, hey?" Theo asked, causing Dean to stop once again.

"Yes."

"That's pretty close to the railway tracks." Theo turned toward them. "The sound of the trains doesn't bother you?"

Dean shrugged. "You get used to it."

Theo smiled as he turned back to Dean. The expression was really starting to creep Dean out. "I'll bet you do," Theo said. "In fact, I'll bet you're pretty fascinated with trains, living so close to them and all."

"Not really," Dean said. "I've never even—"

"What about grain elevators?" Theo asked.

Dean swallowed hard. "W-what about them?"

"I'll bet you'd like to see the town get rid of those ugly old things, wouldn't you? That'd put an end to all the racket the trains make when they stop here, loading their cars with grain at all hours of the day and night."

"Like I said, I've grown up with it, so I don't even notice the sound."

"So, you like the grain elevators then," Theo said. "You'd like them to stay."

"I didn't say that. But I don't have anything against them."

"Are you much of an archer, Dean?"

Dean cleared his throat, alarmed at the sudden change in topic. "Excuse me?"

"You know," Theo pretended to shoot an arrow. "Robin Hood, William Tell, that sort of thing."

"I don't know. We do an archery unit in school every year in gym class, but—hey, wait a second, how did you know my name?"

"Are you any good?" Theo asked, ignoring Dean's question.

"I placed second in the archery competition last spring." Despite his suspicions, Dean couldn't resist the opportunity to brag.

"Did you now," Theo said, his eyes flashing with interest. "And who placed first?"

"One of my best friends, Matt Taylor. Why?"

"So, you and Matt Taylor placed first and second in the archery competition last spring, and you both like the grain elevators. Is that right?"

Not waiting for Dean to respond, Theo opened the hatchback on his car and reached inside, pulling out the arrow with the string tied around it that had punctured his tire. "Is this the kind of arrow you use at school?" Before Dean could reply, Theo shoved it into Dean's hands.

Dean examined the arrow and then quickly handed it back. He didn't like the direction their conversation was taking. He glanced at his watch. "I'm sorry, Mr. Hickenlooper, but I—"

"Call me Theo."

"Theo. Anyway, uh, my mom needs me home to do some yard work, so if everything's okay with your tire—"

"Oh, everything's okay with my tire," Theo said, smiling as he tapped the arrow on the palm of his left hand. "It was a pleasure to meet you, young man. Here, have a campaign button." He pulled one out of his pocket, tucked the arrow under his armpit, and pinned the button to Dean's T-shirt. "And be sure to tell your parents to vote for me."

"Uh, yeah, I will," Dean said, recoiling slightly at Theo's touch. As soon as Theo was finished, Dean pedaled away as fast as he could.

Theo stood beside his car and watched Dean go. Then he turned to a nearby clump of lilac bushes. "Did you get all that?"

Lucy emerged from the bushes as she brushed leaves from her hair, video camera in hand. "You bet I did."

"Think you can make something of it?"

She smiled wickedly. "Just you wait and see."

Theo watched her squeeze into her bright yellow 1980 Dodge Colt and drive off. He shook his head in admiration. "A woman after my own heart."

He grabbed his blazer off the side mirror, then threw it and the arrow onto the passenger seat and got in.

The moment his car disappeared around the corner, Bill stepped out of a clump of caragana bushes on the opposite side of the street, video camera in hand.

18

THE GREAT DEBATE

Matt paced nervously, dressed in a suit and tie with his hair slicked back. Chad and Andrew were similarly garbed and looked just as nervous. The only person who didn't betray even a hint of anxiety as he waited to go on-stage for the mayoral debate was Mayor Bondar. He just sat calmly on a metal folding chair in a room backstage at the community hall reviewing the information on his index cards.

"I just wish we had more time to go over the financial projections for all those revenue-generating ideas we came up with," Matt said. "Are you sure you have those down?"

Mayor Bondar sat back in his chair and smiled as he tapped his right temple. "It's all right up here. And if it's not, I have it here," he said, indicating his cue cards.

"Good." Matt nodded as he continued to pace. "If you still can't find it, I have a copy of your index cards here." He pulled them out of his blazer's inside pocket. "If you need anything, just give me a signal. Are you any good at lip reading?" He mouthed a few words to test the mayor's skills.

"Did you just ask him if his fly was open?" Chad asked.

"Lip reading won't be necessary," Mayor Bondar said,

though he did check his zipper, just in case. "After all, this isn't my first rodeo—far from it! The only person who should be sweating right now is Theo. Facts are important, but when it comes to debates like these, feelings are what matter most. And as far as I know, Theo's never had one! The goal is to make the audience feel good about me, about themselves, and about the future of this town. All I need to do is project confidence, goodwill, honesty, and competence, and we'll have this thing in the bag."

"I admire your poise, sir," Matt said, still pacing.

Mayor Bondar smiled. "With a campaign team like you boys, how could I go wrong?"

Matt allowed himself a tight-lipped grin. "Thank you, sir." He checked his watch. "Speaking of team, where the heck is Dean? We're five minutes out, and he still hasn't shown."

Right on cue, Dean burst into the room, his necktie askew and a sheen of sweat on his forehead. "Guys, Mr. Mayor, we have a problem!"

"Whoa, whoa, whoa, you can't bring that negative energy in here," Matt said, holding out his hands to silence Dean as he approached him. "The mayor's about to go on stage."

"That's exactly why I need to talk to him," Dean protested.

"Whatever it is, it can wait until after the debate," Matt said, shepherding Dean toward the door.

"No, it can't," Dean said, pushing against him. "It's—"

"Mayor Bondar?" The boys stopped their struggle as Otto Nimigeers, editor and publisher of the *Milligan Creek Review*, poked his head in the door, looking askance at the tussling boys. Otto was serving as the moderator of the debate. As the newspaper editor, it was assumed he would be the most impartial. "We're ready for you now."

"But I still haven't—"

"Whatever it is, Dean, don't worry about it," Mayor Bondar said, clapping a meaty hand on the boy's shoulder. "Just watch and learn, boys. Watch and learn."

"Go get 'im, Mr. Mayor!" Matt said, pumping his fist as he and the other boys watched the mayor go out. The minute he was gone, Matt turned on Dean. "What the heck are you doing coming in here with your pants on fire like that? You want to throw him off his game?"

"If you'd just let me finish, I can tell you!"

"No time for that," Matt said. "I don't want to miss a second of this. Theo is about to go down in flames, and I want to see every last spark." He pushed past Dean and went out.

"What's going on?" Chad asked as he and Andrew converged on Dean.

"My parents had the news on right before I left," Dean said. "And you'll never guess whose face was on TV."

"Whose?" Chad asked.

Dean jabbed his thumb at his own chest. "Mine!"

The other two boys looked at him in confusion. "What?" they exclaimed in unison.

Out on stage, Otto was in the midst of introducing the two candidates. He sat at a table between their two podiums, a gavel, a glass of water, and a microphone in front of him. ". . . and on my left is a man who needs no introduction to the people of this town, Mayor Michael Bondar." The audience clapped. Some people cheered, but a few boos were mixed in.

"What the heck are those boos all about?" Matt asked as Chad, Andrew, and Dean joined him in the front row.

133

"I'll tell you after the debate," Chad whispered, realizing the boys' arrival in the hall had prompted a number of stares, pointing fingers, and whispers.

"That can't be good," Dean muttered, seeing a number of angry gazes directed his way. "Apparently, other people saw the news too."

"What news?" Matt asked.

"Just keep a low profile," Andrew whispered. "Like you said, we don't want to distract the mayor."

Onstage, Theo looked remarkably confident, as if he felt like he already had the debate in hand.

Backstage, Rudy was wearing a ball cap twisted sideways, sunglasses, and fake gold chains around his neck as he rehearsed his lines, ready to bust out his Hickenlooper rap when Theo gave him the go-ahead.

"With the introductions out of the way, it's time for each candidate's opening statement," Otto said. "In keeping with tradition, we will start with the incumbent, Mayor Bondar, and then his opponent, Councilor Theo Hickenlooper. Each candidate will be given ten minutes. Mayor Bondar, if you please."

Mayor Bondar cleared his throat and straightened his tie, taking a moment to shuffle his index cards before he looked up at the audience. Then he broke into a huge smile. "Good evening! It's a pleasure to be able to address you all tonight. I've been mayor of this town for so long that probably the last thing any of you want to hear from me tonight is another speech. Anyone? Anyone?" He got a few strained laughs and pained smiles in response to yet another Ben Stein impersonation. "Anyway, tonight I thought I'd break from tradition and . . . uh . . . and uh . . ."

"What's going on?" Matt asked, seeing the distracted look on Mayor Bondar's face as his voice trailed off and he stared at the back of the hall.

Chad raised himself slightly out of his seat and turned to look just in time to see Staff Sergeant Romanowski direct two constables to walk down the aisles on opposite sides of the room while he walked up the middle. Right behind them was none other than Tucker Butker and Bill, the cameraman, filming the action. Chad plunked back down into his chair. "The police! They're coming!"

"The police? Coming for who?" Matt asked.

"Us!" Chad hissed, already getting out of his chair. "Who do you think? Come on!"

"But the debate! Mayor Bondar, I don't want to—"

"Just come!" Chad said, pulling him along as Dean and Andrew followed.

The boys burst out the side door into the orange evening light.

"Would someone please tell me what the heck is going on?" Matt pleaded.

"No time for that," Chad said. "Run!"

19

FUGITIVES

"Where should we go?" Andrew asked as the boys ran north, putting a strip of trees between themselves and the community hall to conceal them from any pursuers.

"How about Dean's house?" Chad said. "It's the closest place."

"Which means it's the first place they'll look," Andrew pointed out.

"Yeah, and once my parents saw that news story, they went ballistic and confined me to my room," Dean said, huffing as he ran. "I had to sneak out my window just to get here to warn you guys."

Matt slowed to a jog and then stopped. "Okay, that does it. I'm not taking one more step until someone tells me what the heck is going on."

"But Matt, the police—"

"I don't care about the police," Matt said, silencing Dean. "They'll catch us sooner or later no matter what we do. Now tell me, what happened?"

"Theo framed me," Dean said, bending over and putting his hands on his knees as he struggled to catch his breath. "I ran into him the other day on the way home from meeting with Mayor Bondar. He asked me some questions and showed me the arrow that punctured his tire. I never thought to tell you guys about it because it was just a weird encounter. He knew my name and everything, even though we'd never met before. Anyway, it turns out someone was filming us, and then they edited things together to make it look like I confessed that you and I were the ones who shot the arrow into his tire and put up that banner between the grain elevators."

"But we did do those things," Matt said. "Wait a second, how did my name get mixed up in this?"

"It's a long story," Dean said. "The point is, they aired the story tonight on the news, right before the debate. They used it to smear Mayor Bondar, saying his campaign had been run by criminals. Obviously, the police saw it, and they came into the community hall to arrest us."

Matt took a moment to absorb the news. Then he started running. The others hurried to catch up. "Matt, where are you going?" Chad asked.

"To the tie fort!"

"The tie fort? But we haven't been there for years."

"Exactly," Matt said. "It's one of the last places they'll look."

Thirty minutes later, the boys piled into a fort that they had constructed from old railway ties, which had been left behind when the rail line replaced them a few years earlier. The ties were cut in six-foot and two-foot lengths, which made them light enough for the boys to lift and also made them perfect building blocks. The fort was located a couple of miles east of town, concealed in a stand of trees beside the tracks. To the best of the boys' knowledge, the railway workers didn't even know it was there, though they were likely confused when they came to pick up the discarded ties, and several dozen of them were missing. The fort was eight feet wide and twelve feet long, and it even featured a second floor. Until they built the tree house at the Taylors' farm, it had been their primary hangout, though Dean always claimed he was allergic to the faint smell of tar that still clung to the ties.

"So, what do we do now?" Chad asked as he brushed away a few cobwebs before taking a seat.

"You know, I'm actually impressed this thing is still standing," Andrew said, taking a moment to admire the construction.

"Forget about that," Dean said. "We're about to go to jail!"

"You're not going to jail," Matt replied.

"Oh yeah?" Dean turned toward him. "How can you be so sure?"

"Because I'm going to confess to everything."

The other boys looked at him in disbelief.

"You're what?" Chad asked.

"It was my idea from the beginning, and I dragged you guys into it, so it's only fitting that I take the blame." Matt eyes scoured the fort's dirt floor. "There's no point in the rest of you ruining your lives."

"But they'll never believe you did it alone," Andrew said. "It's not even possible logistically."

"He's right," Dean said. "Besides, we all just ran out of the community hall like a bunch of rats deserting a sinking ship. If the police didn't believe we were guilty before that, now they know for sure. The same goes for everyone else in town."

"I'll just tell them you guys were worried about me. That you were covering for me."

139

Dean sat back and puffed out his cheeks, letting out a long, slow breath as he shook his head. "I don't know, Matt. I've seen how the police interrogate people on TV. If there's any inconsistency in our stories, they'll find it, and then we'll be in even more trouble for lying about it."

"Dean's right," Chad said. "Besides, you may have pushed us to do it, but we could have backed out at any time. We all chose to help you, so we should all take the fall. And never mind the police. Are you going to lie to Mom and Dad on top of everything and say I wasn't involved? Do you really think they'll believe you, after all the crazy things we've done together?"

"I'm with Chad," Andrew said. "We did this together, so we should pay for it together. Besides, look on the bright side. Maybe the publicity over our arrest will actually help save the elevators. If people realize young people like us care so much that we're willing to take the law into our own hands to save them, maybe they'll think twice about making the deal with Fortitude."

Matt's eyes lit up. "That's a great point! People break laws all the time to protest things they don't like—nuclear weapons, cruelty to animals, air pollution—and other people don't look at them as criminals. They see them as heroes. Maybe that's how people will see us."

"Well, my mom definitely won't see me as a hero," Dean said. "You neither, Matt."

"I'm talking about normal people, Dean. And no offense, but your mom definitely does not fit into that category."

"None taken," Dean said as he and the other boys laughed, which released a bit of their anxiety. "I couldn't agree more."

Two hours later, Staff Sergeant Romanowski was gathered around a TV set with his two constables, laughing and drinking coffee as they pointed at the screen. Just then the doorbell on the police station sounded. Still chuckling, Romanowski went to answer it. He found Matt, Chad, Dean, and Andrew waiting outside, their hands against the wall, their legs spread, and their heads bowed, like a group of criminals waiting to be arrested. His set down his coffee cup and hastily unlocked the door.

"Dean Muller and Matt Taylor, exactly the boys I wanted to see. But why are you standing against the wall like that?"

"Once we heard the news, we figured we might as well come down here and get it over with," Matt said.

"I'm glad you did," Romanowski replied. "In fact, I was about to write up my report right now, and I have a few questions I'd like you to answer."

"No matter what they are, the answer is yes," Matt said.

The staff sergeant raised his eyebrows in surprise. "So, you want to press charges then?"

His hands still pinned against the wall, Matt looked over his shoulder in confusion. "Excuse me?" The other boys appeared just as baffled.

"Against Theo Hickenlooper, for framing you and Dean."

Matt pulled away from the wall and exchanged a look with the other boys, then turned to face Romanowski. "I'm sorry, sir, but I don't understand."

"You did see the news story, didn't you?"

"No, but—"

"I mean the second news story, the one that showed the complete uncut exchange between Mr. Hickenlooper and Dean?"

Matt shook his head, as if trying to clear it of bewildering images. "I'm sorry, Staff Sergeant, there was a second news story?"

"Yes. Where have you guys been for the last couple of hours? They even interrupted an episode of Growing Pains to show it."

"Joyce isn't going to be happy about that," Dean muttered.

"We arrested Theo right there on stage at the debate, and the guys from Channel Six were on location to capture it. I figured it was only fair, seeing as they were the ones who gave us the tip. We even brought in Hickenlooper's campaign manager, Rudy Bricksaw, on suspicion of him being an accomplice. He was certainly dressed like a criminal—wearing sunglasses at night, no less, his cap on sideways, not to mention all those chains—but after questioning him, we let him go. However, if you boys know anything that could change that . . ."

"So when you came into the community hall earlier tonight, you weren't coming for us?" Matt asked.

Romanowski balked at the idea. "No, why would we?"

"No reason," Chad said hastily, looking behind Romanowski as laughter erupted from the office.

The staff sergeant glanced behind him. "Oh, the guys recorded the story and are probably watching it again right now. Why don't you come in and see it?"

Sharing silent looks of relief and surprise, the boys followed Romanowski past the reception desk and into the main office area.

"Rewind that tape, Chambers," Romanowski said. "We

have some surprise guests who want to see you fine young men in action."

"Sure thing, boss." Constable Chambers rewound the video and then pressed "play." The boys watched in wonder as Tucker narrated a news story over top of a split screen that showed the original story of Dean and Theo talking alongside uncut footage of their exchange. Then the scene cut to the constables marching onto the stage and slapping handcuffs on Theo in front of the shocked audience, followed by footage of Mounties doing the same to Lucy at the Channel Six News office. It turns out she had edited and aired the story before Bill could stop her, so he teamed up with Tucker to expose her and Theo's plot.

"It may seem like a dark day for journalistic integrity," Tucker said, wrapping things up, "not to mention small-town politics, but like anything in life, journalism and politics are neutral forces, capable of the highest good and the darkest evil. It's men and women like you and me who decide how to wield such power, and this is one reporter who has decided to use his power for good. This is Tucker Butker, live, loud, and on location in Milligan Creek."

"Wait a second," Chad said once the news story ended. "If you guys arrested Theo, that means . . ."

"Mayor Bondar won!" Matt exclaimed.

Staff Sergeant Romanowski nodded as he wiped drops of coffee from his mustache. "That's right. At least he won the debate, not that either of them got a chance to present their arguments. As for the election, unless another candidate throws their hat into the ring at the last minute, I'd say he'll win by a landslide. No one's going to vote for Theo after tonight."

A few minutes later, the boys burst out of the police station, bubbling with excitement. They had agreed not to press charges against Theo. Not only did they not want him to get into any more trouble than he already was, they also didn't want the police to investigate the arrow incident any further, knowing the finger of blame would eventually point back at them.

"Can you believe it?" Matt said. "I can't wait to congratulate Mayor Bondar!"

"Me too," Andrew replied. "Though in a way, it's too bad things turned out like this. Think about all the work we put into his campaign. I would have loved to see that debate."

"And the arrest," Chad added.

"It was still worth it," Matt said. "Think about all we learned in the process."

"Yeah, I learned one thing for sure," Chad said, putting his arm around Dean's shoulders. "It never would have happened if it weren't for our wild card here."

Dean grinned in gratitude as the other boys echoed Chad's praise.

20

BONDAR DROPS A BOMB

The following morning, the boys couldn't wait to get to Mayor Bondar's office and congratulate him on his win. Chad, Matt, and Andrew rode their bikes to Dean's house, where they found him halfway out the front door arguing with his mother.

"But Mom, the news story said we didn't have anything to do with the arrow incident, that Theo tried to frame us. Remember?"

"I know, but I still think there's something fishy about it."

"But Mrs. Muller, we were all sleeping over at your house the night it happened," Matt called out. "You saw us with your own eyes."

She looked up at Matt as he and the other boys approached the open front door. "Don't try confusing me with the facts, Matt Taylor. I still haven't decided whether or not you're an alien, let alone innocent."

"Mommm . . ." Dean said, edging out the door.

"Okay, you can go," she said. "If the police say you're innocent, I guess that's good enough for me. But I'm watching you boys, especially you, Matt. And if you are an alien, don't even think about trying to take over our planet. If you do, you'll have to go through me first."

"I wouldn't dare, Mrs. Muller," Matt said, grinning despite himself as he and the other boys leaped onto their bikes, "even if I was an alien, which I'm not!"

When the boys reached the town office, they threw their bikes into the bike rack and raced inside.

"Good morning, Mrs. Chaykowski," Matt said, breezing past Rose's desk with the other boys. "We're just here to congratulate—"

"Hold your horses, boys," Rose said as Matt put his hand on the doorknob to Mayor Bondar's office. "He's in a meeting."

"Oh," Matt said, backing off. "We can wait." He and the other boys sat down in the waiting area, taking in the rustic décor, which included several oil paintings of prairie landscapes donated by a local artist. "The mayor must be pretty excited after last night," Matt said.

Rose smiled. "He is. And I'm sure he'll be eager to thank you boys for the role you played. In fact, Dean, I should get your autograph. You're kind of a celebrity now after all that news coverage."

"Cool!" Dean said, standing up and taking the pen and notepad Rose held out to him. He went to sign his name and then hesitated. "Wait a second, I've never given an autograph before. How do you do it?"

"Just write your name," Chad said. "The way you normally would."

"Or if that's too hard, you can just write a big X," Matt suggested.

"Very funny," Dean said, his forehead furrowed in concentration as he signed his name with a flourish. "There you are." He handed the notepad and pen back to Rose.

"So, who's the mayor meeting with?" Matt asked. "Seems kind of early to—"

Just then the door to the mayor's office opened, revealing Mayor Bondar's smiling face. "Hello, boys," he said. "Be with you in a minute." He turned back to his office as he opened the door further to allow his guests to leave. "It's been a pleasure, gentlemen," he said, shaking their hands. "I look forward to working with you in the future."

When the two visitors saw the boys, their faces lit up in recognition. "Hey, it's the kid from TV," one of them said, pointing at Dean and then shaking his hand. "Nice to meet you, son."

"Nice to meet you too . . ." Dean said, appearing as if he were in a daze. Like the other boys, all he could see was the green Fortitude logo emblazoned on the men's matching white jackets.

They watched the men go, then turned back to Mayor Bondar, who grinned at them as he stood in the doorway to his office. "Well, don't just stand there, come in, come in!" He stood back and gestured for them to enter.

Mayor Bondar had hardly closed the door behind them when Matt erupted. "Mayor Bondar, I don't understand. Why were the Fortitude guys here? Last night, the debate, I thought you won. That means—"

"Why don't you all have a seat?" Mayor Bondar said. "And I'll explain."

The boys did as he asked, though Matt sat right on the edge of his chair, ready to spring to his feet in protest at the earliest opportunity.

Mayor Bondar walked around his desk and sank down into his plush swivel office chair, taking a deep breath and letting it out before he began. "We fought a good fight, boys, and we taught Theo and this town an important lesson.

Winning is important, but it isn't everything, and it's definitely not worth sacrificing your reputation to do it."

Matt opened his mouth to respond, but Mayor Bondar held up his right index finger to indicate he wasn't finished. "But I also learned an important lesson through this experience. No matter how much I want something to be true, no matter how much I'd like our way of life to continue as it is, to keep things the way they are, the only thing in life that's constant is change. If we don't remain open to new things or adapt to new circumstances, we die. That's just as true for communities as it is for individual people or animals living in the wild. It's evolution, the law of the jungle."

"But . . . this . . . isn't . . . the jungle, Mayor Bondar," Matt said. "It's the prairies. Saskatchewan. The rules are different here."

Mayor Bondar shook his head slowly. "I'm sorry to say it, but they're not. We may not have literal lions or tigers or hyenas lurking around here, but we have different kinds of predators, and the law of the jungle still applies: eat or be eaten, kill or be killed."

Matt shook his head in confusion. "I still don't understand. What does this have to do with Fortitude?"

"If we don't accept Fortitude's offer, they're going to take it to the next town down the road. And if they do that, Milligan Creek is finished," Mayor Bondar said, "because then that town will become a major center, not us. Furthermore, since Fortitude last made an offer, they have sweetened the deal considerably. While I remain personally opposed to the idea, as mayor, I have to act in the best interest of my community, and no matter which way I look at it, if we want to keep Milligan Creek on the map, Fortitude is our only hope."

The room fell silent as Mayor Bondar gave the boys some time to digest his surprising reversal. "The good news is, you boys have injected lots of creative thinking into all sorts of areas in this town in terms of cutting costs and raising revenues, and I plan to implement many of your ideas—giving you full credit, of course."

"And the grain elevators?" Matt asked, swallowing hard. "What happens to them?"

Mayor Bondar's face dimmed somewhat. "According to the timeline Fortitude has proposed, by this time next year, they'll be gone."

A few minutes later, the boys silently reclaimed their bikes from the rack outside the town office.

Chad held his bike by the handlebars, staring at the ground, then he looked up at the others. "What do we do now?"

"I don't know about you guys, but I was thinking about heading downtown to see if anyone else wants my autograph," Dean said.

"I mean about the elevators." Chad turned to his brother. "Matt, it's not like you to be so silent. What are you thinking?"

Matt threw a leg over his bike. "I'm thinking if Mayor Bondar won't save the elevators, then it's up to us."

"No way," Dean said. "We narrowly avoided being arrested the last time. There's no way I'm going near those things again."

"I hate to say it, but I agree," Andrew said. "As Mayor Bondar said, no matter how much you want something to be true, sometimes you just have to accept things as they are."

Matt looked at Chad for support, but all he could do

was shrug. "What else can we do, Matt? You heard the mayor. It's practically a done deal."

"Maybe for you it is," Matt said, hopping onto his bike and pedaling away. "But he also said this is a jungle, and I'm not about to let myself—or this town—get eaten."

21

Matt's Secret

"Again!" Matt said, ringing the bell at the top of the climbing tower and then leaning back and pushing away from the wall with his legs, speeding his way to the bottom as Chad belayed him.

"Again?" Chad said as Matt's feet touched down on the crash pad. "But that's your sixth time in a row."

Matt stood at the bottom of the tower looking up, his face resolute as he grasped two handholds. "On belay?"

Chad sighed. "Belay on, I guess, although some of us have better things to do."

The brothers were out at the climbing wall on their own. In return for Matt agreeing to polish the gym floor for a week, Mr. Karky had given them permission to do some extra climbing after school.

Matt clambered up the tower, ignoring his brother's complaints. He purposely chose the most difficult route, pushing himself to stretch and even leap between handholds. He completed the route in near record time once again, though he paused at the top after ringing the bell.

"Had enough?" Chad asked, squinting up at him and shielding his eyes from the fading afternoon sun.

Matt nodded, huffing with exertion as he took in the view. "For today." This time instead of rappelling down in a normal fashion, he turned around and literally walked down the wall as Chad belayed him, flipping around at the last instant and planting his feet on the crash pad. Without hesitation, he started to unbuckle his climbing harness.

"What's your hurry all of a sudden?" Chad asked as he wound the climbing rope around his arm.

"Can you put the gear away today?" Matt asked, shimmying out of his harness as it fell to the ground. He took off his helmet and handed it and the harness to Chad, who struggled to take them as he continued to wind the rope. "I need to get to the hardware store before it closes."

Chad frowned. "The hardware store? What for?"

"Can't a man have some secrets?" Matt asked, already hurrying away.

"You're not a man!" Chad called after him. "You're my brother. And my younger brother at that," he muttered. "Speaking of which, why am I putting the climbing gear away—again?" He looked up. "Hey, Matt, get back—"

But Matt was already gone.

That night at supper, Matt was uncharacteristically silent as he ate. Chad eyed him suspiciously as he passed the mashed potatoes to his father. Joyce was away at a dance practice.

"So, boys, learn anything interesting at school today?" Mrs. Taylor asked as she served herself some green beans, which they had grown in their garden that summer.

"Only that my brother is turning into some sort of climbing freak," Chad said. "And that he doesn't like to clean up after himself, though that's nothing unusual."

"I'm so glad you boys are enjoying that climbing wall," Mrs. Taylor replied. "Something told me it would be a big hit."

Matt continued to eat silently, his eyes on his plate.

"You know, if we had one of those things back in my day, I would have turned out to be quite a climber too," Mr. Taylor said. "It's all about upper-body strength, and I've always had plenty of that," he added, flexing his bicep.

"Oh honey," Mrs. Taylor said, laughing. "You could never be a rock climber. You're afraid of heights."

"What do you mean?" Mr. Taylor asked. "I am a pilot, after all." In addition to flying for fun, he also had a spray plane business.

"That's different," Mrs. Taylor said. "You're inside a machine, so it feels like you're in control. Back here on the ground, you get dizzy every time I ask you to climb a stepladder."

"Did you ever think that might be my clever way of getting out of chores?"

Mrs. Taylor arched an eyebrow. "Oh really? If you're so clever, why did you just admit it?"

Mr. Taylor was about to respond when Matt stood up. "May I be excused?"

His parents looked at him in surprise. "Is everything alright?" Mrs. Taylor asked.

Matt rolled his shoulders and stretched his arms. "Yeah, I'm just a little sore from all those times up and down the wall. I think I'll lie down for a while."

"Me too," Chad said, standing up. "I mean, I think I'll rest for a bit too." He held up his hands in response to his parents' questioning looks. "What? Belaying is a lot harder than it looks."

Chad found Matt on his bed facing the wall. Chad stood in the doorway and folded his arms across his chest. "Are you going to tell me what you're up to or what?"

"No."

"Why not?"

Matt rolled over and looked at his brother. "Because I don't want to get anyone else in trouble—that and apparently everyone else is just fine with Fortitude wiping our elevators, not to mention our town, off the map."

Chad sighed. "Matt, we've been over this, and—"

"And I know exactly what you're going to say, so don't bother. And please turn out the light. I was serious when I said I needed some rest."

Chad took a deep breath, then flicked off the light. "Fine," he said, as he pulled the door shut. "If you change your mind, I'm going to see what's on TV."

The moment Chad was gone, Matt grabbed a small travel alarm clock from his nightstand and set it for 3:00 a.m. Then he closed his eyes and tried to force himself to fall asleep.

§

At 3:05 a.m. the following morning, Chad tossed and turned in bed, caught in the grip of a horrible dream. He had been belaying Matt up the climbing wall, but then the entire climbing wall buckled and fell, and Matt plunged to the ground, screaming in horror. Just before the climbing wall crushed them both, Chad woke up.

He sat up, his body covered in a sheen of sweat, and looked over at Matt's bed. It was empty. Chad was just about to get up and see if Matt had gone to the bathroom when he noticed the curtains fluttering in the breeze. Their window was open. He walked over to it and looked out, then shut it when he saw no sign of his brother outside, goose bumps rising on his arms in the cool breeze.

"What the heck is that crazy kid up to now?" he muttered. He climbed back into bed, threw his covers over himself, and flopped onto his side.

After lying there for a moment, he sat up again. "Aw, who am I kidding?" He got out of bed, threw on some warm clothes, and then slipped out of his bedroom, grabbing his gloves and a toque on his way out of the house.

22

THE CLIMBER

"Looking toward Saturday, get ready for the return of summer!" Tucker said as he stood in front of a weather map, his image projected on the TV that sat on the counter in Dean's kitchen. Tucker was filling in for Channel Six's weatherman, Chuck Peters, who was out with laryngitis. Dean watched the broadcast as he shoveled Honeycomb cereal into his mouth, having woken up late for school.

"That's right, folks," Tucker continued. "I realize it's nearly October, but we're going to get a quick warming trend before temperatures plunge again, which means we could also be looking at some thundershowers before the weekend is through. Maybe even a tornado in southern areas once the cold and warm air masses collide, so I don't know whether to tell you to break out the sunscreen or batten down the hatches. Sandy?"

The broadcast cut to Channel Six's anchorwoman, Sandy Reynolds, her smiling lips glistening from a new layer of lipstick that had been hastily applied while Tucker was delivering the weather report. "Thank you, Tucker. And on a sad note, it's my duty to inform our viewers that this is your last day with us. You're off to bigger and better things, I understand."

The camera cut back to Tucker, who rose up and down on his toes, his body rippling with excitement. "That's right, Sandy. I'm heading to Channel Twelve's provincial broadcast out of Saskatoon, starting next week."

"Going over to the enemy, are you?" Sandy said, giving him a teasing smile. "Well, you'll be missed, but we're happy to see you moving up in the world. Finally, in other local news . . ."

Dean stopped listening when he heard a knock at the door. "I'll get it," he called out to his mother, who was somewhere in the house, his father having left early for work.

When he opened the door, he was surprised to find Chad on his doorstep, still dressed in his warm clothing from the night before, including his toque and gloves.

"Chad," Dean said, his mouth full of Honeycomb, having carried his cereal bowl to the door. "I take it you didn't hear the forecast. It's calling for summer weather, not winter."

Chad pulled off his toque and stepped inside. "Forget about that, we've got a bigger problem."

"Oh yeah, what's that?" Dean said, shoveling another spoonful of cereal into his mouth.

"It's Matt. I think he may have finally gone off the deep end."

"Finally? I thought he lived in the deep end."

"I'm serious, Dean."

"Oh yeah? What did he do now?"

"You need to come and see for yourself."

Minutes later, the boys skidded their bikes to a stop beside the grain elevators. A crowd had already gathered at the base of one of Fortitude's elevators.

"What the heck's going on?" Dean asked as he and Chad threw down their bikes and walked around to the front of the elevators.

"You'll see," Chad said.

When Dean rounded the corner, he stopped short, unable to believe his eyes. Suspended from the side of the elevator, about twenty feet from the top, was a platform made of canvas and a metal frame. Seated on it was Matt. Hanging down from the platform was a banner that said, "Save Our Elevators, Save Our Town!" The words were written vertically rather than horizontally, unlike their previous banner. It also had weights on the bottom to ensure it hung straight down.

"Oh no," Dean said. "Now they're going to know for sure it was us who hung the first banner."

"Not necessarily," Chad replied. "They could just assume that Matt's a copycat."

"Good thing we had Andrew make the first banner," Dean said. "His handwriting is different." He turned and looked at Chad as an idea struck him. "Wait a second, you told me we have a problem. You mean you didn't know he was going to do this?"

Chad shook his head. "Not a clue. He's been acting strange the last few days, and he's been climbing like a madman, but I had no idea he was going to do something this drastic. I should have followed him to the hardware store the other day. I guess he was reading up on climbing, and he bought some hardware that he used to create that platform and some anchors, which he screwed into the elevator as he climbed, so he wouldn't need anyone to belay him."

"You mean he climbed all the way up there by himself, at night?"

Chad nodded. "Yup."

Dean stared up at Matt in wonder. "He's braver than I thought. Or crazier. Why didn't he just use the man lift, like you did before?"

"After the arrow stunt, they did a better job of securing the doors. They're locked up as tight as a drum."

Dean shook his head as he continued to look at Matt. "That's amazing. He's got guts. I'll give him that."

"Guts, yes," Chad said. "Brains? I'm not so—" He was interrupted by the chirp of a police siren. The boys looked behind them as a cruiser pulled up, the crowd parting to let it through. Chad's face flushed with worry. "Uh-oh . . ."

"Tell me about it," Dean said.

Chad shook his head. "My parents are going to kill him."

Just then, Andrew skidded up on his bike. "Holy cow!" he said, craning his head to look up at Matt. "So, it's true!"

"How did you hear about it so fast?" Chad asked, turning to him.

"As soon as I pulled up to the school, everyone was talking about it," Andrew said. "Some of the buses pass by here, and they saw him on the way in."

"He is so dead," Dean said as he watched Romanowski get out of his car and approach the base of the elevator, shielding his eyes as he looked up.

"What seems to be the problem, son?" Romanowski called up to Matt.

In response, Matt pulled out a megaphone.

"Man, he thought of everything!" Dean whispered.

"I'm not coming down until Fortitude agrees to save our grain elevators," Matt said. "I'm officially on a hunger strike too. Without these elevators, Milligan Creek

160

is going to wither up and die, so if the elevators go, I'm going too."

Romanowski continued looking up at Matt for a few seconds, then sighed, shook his head, and walked back to his car. He pulled out the mic for his CB radio as he leaned one elbow on his cruiser's roof. "Ruth, can you get Marty on the phone? Looks like we're going to need the ladder truck over at the grain elevators."

"Roger that," Ruth replied. Marty was the chief of Milligan Creek's fire department, which had purchased a new ladder truck earlier that year—the same truck they had used to take down the boys' first banner.

"It's not going to work," Andrew whispered.

"What do you mean?" Chad asked.

"Count the boards," Andrew said. "Each one is a foot high. The ladder on that fire truck only extends one hundred feet. Matt's platform is at one hundred and five feet."

"Man, he really did think of everything!" Dean said, pointing at the boards as he counted them silently, then quickly lost his place. He turned to Andrew. "Hey, how'd you count them so fast?"

"Easy, I started at the top," Andrew said. "The elevator's one hundred and twenty-five feet tall."

"Oh," Dean said, moving his lips silently as he used his finger to count each board.

"Speaking of which, if the fire truck doesn't work, they could always get at him from the top," Andrew suggested.

Chad shook his head. "Nope. Matt told me earlier that he screwed the roof hatch shut. Besides, even if they break it open, what are they going to do? I can't see anyone rappelling down to get him. No one knows how, and besides, it's too dangerous. Even if they can get to him, they can't exactly tie him up and drag him inside."

The three boys stood in silence, staring up at Matt. "How long do you suppose he plans to stay up there?" Dean asked.

"He said he has enough water to last him a week," Chad said.

Andrew turned to him. "Did he mention how he plans to go to the bathroom?"

Chad grinned. "That's one detail he might have missed."

"Oh boy," Dean said, looking around at the growing crowd. "With everyone watching and everything."

A short time later, the fire truck arrived, but as Andrew predicted, the ladder wasn't quite long enough to reach Matt. Even though Romanowski himself climbed to the top and tried to reason with Matt, he refused to budge.

Following the failure of the ladder truck, firefighters broke through the roof hatch and lowered a rope and harness to Matt, urging him to put it on, so they could pull him up, but he refused that too, though he did accept some additional water, which they lowered down to him.

With the crowd growing, Romanowski had his constables create a perimeter in case anything fell from above. Then he called in Matt and Chad's parents, hoping they could talk some sense into their son. But no matter how much they threatened or cajoled him; he wouldn't budge. Not even Fiona could get him to change his mind.

"I hate to say it, but I admire his determination," Joyce said afterwards as she gazed up at Matt alongside her mother.

"Don't tell your father, but so do I," Mrs. Taylor whispered. Mr. Taylor was much more upset about his son's stunt, worried about the effect it might have on his spray plane business. Soon the entire crowd, which continued to grow throughout the day, was split along similar lines, with some for and some against what Matt was doing.

Midway through the day, Mayor Bondar took a crack at trying to talk Matt down, going up to the top of the extension ladder to meet with him face to face. But Mayor Bondar was the last person Matt wanted to see. He felt like the mayor had betrayed him and the other boys personally by making a last-minute deal with Fortitude.

As darkness fell, the crowd dwindled somewhat, though a handful of people in both camps remained, including Matt's parents, who brought in their truck camper to sleep for the night. The police also set up spotlights to illuminate Matt and to prevent him from sleeping, thinking it might wear him down faster. But Matt had anticipated that outcome as well and put a sleeping mask over his eyes before settling in for the night.

"What do we do now, chief?" Constable Chambers asked as Romanowski adjusted one of the spotlights to ensure it was aimed properly.

"We wait," Romanowski said, standing up and looking at Matt, his hands on his hips. "He's a kid. He's probably scared, tired, cold, and hungry. He won't last long."

Over by their pup tent, which Chad, Dean, and Andrew had pitched to spend the night, Chad chuckled at the staff sergeant's words. "Clearly, he doesn't know my brother."

23

THE STANDOFF

The following morning, the sky to the east blazed with red right before the sun broke over the horizon. It looked like it was going to be a beautiful day, just like the forecast said. However, anyone familiar with weather on the prairies knew that a red sky in the morning was an ominous sign. It meant moisture-rich clouds were on their way, and despite the clear sky, a change in the weather was imminent. As if to confirm this, a wind had also kicked up overnight, indicating that two air masses with drastically different temperatures were about to collide.

Up on the platform, Matt pried his eyes open. They felt dry and grainy, the result of too little sleep. Despite his bravado—and the fact that he was not only on the platform but also roped in to three anchors screwed into the elevator wall—waves of fear kept hitting him, not to mention undercurrents of doubt about the intelligence of his stunt.

When he first hatched the plan, he knew it was crazy, but it also sounded fun. And once he reached a certain point, there was no way he could back out. However, as the platform bumped gently against the elevator, knocked about by the wind, he started to feel seasick.

It didn't help that he was starving or that every time he looked down he felt dizzy. He took a sip of water, hoping it would settle his stomach.

Down on the ground, Romanowski pulled up to take over for Constable Chambers. A member of the fire crew and the ambulance staff had also stayed on site overnight in case of emergency.

"How's it going?" the staff sergeant asked as he handed Chambers a cup of coffee.

"Thanks, chief. Nothing's changed." He let out a huge yawn, accentuating his mustache, which could easily give Romanowski's a run for its money. "But I'm sure ready to hit the sack."

"Go ahead, you deserve it."

Just then Romanowski spotted Mrs. Taylor emerge from her camper. He walked over to her. "Good morning," he said, giving her a wave as he approached.

"Good morning, Staff Sergeant," she replied, rubbing her upper arms and shivering. "But it's a cold one. I sure hope Matt didn't freeze up there."

They both looked up, and then Romanowski redirected his gaze at Mrs. Taylor. "Get any bright ideas overnight about how to get him down?"

"I'm afraid not. I know Matt. Once he sets his mind on something, there's no stopping him."

Romanowski nodded as he took a sip of coffee. "Well, I put a call in to the SWAT team in Regina. They have a couple of guys who are expert climbers. They agreed to send them up here if we can't talk your boy down before tonight. But I have to warn you, it won't be cheap. And neither the town nor the RCMP is willing to foot the bill."

Mrs. Taylor nodded. "I understand, Staff Sergeant. Let me try to talk to him again."

A few minutes later, Mrs. Taylor relayed the news to Matt through Romanowski's megaphone, but he still wouldn't budge.

"Send the bill to Fortitude!" Matt said. "They can afford it. Besides, I don't need any help getting down. I already said, I'll come down as soon as I have a guarantee that Fortitude won't tear down our elevators!"

Mrs. Taylor handed the megaphone back to Romanowski and sighed. "It was worth a try."

Romanowski held out the megaphone to Chad, who, along with Dean and Andrew, had gathered by Mrs. Taylor. "Want to give it a try?"

Chad laughed. "With all due respect, Staff Sergeant, if he won't listen to her, he definitely won't listen to us."

Romanowski nodded. "Well, like I told your mother, if he doesn't come down on his own by tonight, I'm calling in the SWAT team. We can't let this circus continue. If Matt wants to keep Milligan Creek on the map, this is definitely not the way to do it." He gestured to a couple of satellite news trucks that had joined the vigil, including one from Channel Six.

The weather remained sunny until noon. Clouds rolled in, and the temperature plunged. The wind also picked up, causing Matt's platform to rock even more than before. He used a couple of extra anchors to secure the metal frame more firmly to the wall, which helped a little.

By midafternoon Romanowski's patience was wearing thin. He walked over to the Taylors' camper and knocked on the door. They opened it and invited him to sit with them at the camper's tiny table, where they had just poured themselves some coffee. He politely refused a cup, taking off his hat and rubbing his forehead.

"I know I told you I'd wait until tonight, but I don't like

the look of this weather, and the last thing anyone wants is for your boy to get hurt."

"We understand," Mr. Taylor said. "I'm sorry he's put you through this."

"Well, I can't say I don't admire his guts," Romanowski said, "but enough is enough."

Up on the platform, Matt shivered. He had put on every piece of warm clothing he owned, but the wind still cut through it and his sleeping bag. If he was this cold during the day, he had no idea how he was going to make it through another night. With the temperature still dropping and the wind picking up, including some gusts that billowed his canvas platform like a sail, he was getting genuinely scared. He also didn't want to put his parents—or himself—under the financial burden of paying for the SWAT team.

Just when he was thinking about grabbing his megaphone and calling it quits, he heard a low thumping sound in the distance. There was no mistaking it; a helicopter was approaching. Could it be the SWAT team already? However, when he pulled out his binoculars to look, he saw the words "Channel 12" emblazoned on the chopper's side.

§

"This is Tucker Butker coming at you live, loud, and on location in the Channel Twelve News chopper just above the town of Milligan Creek, where we're into day two of a classic David and Goliath standoff between—whoa!" Tucker grabbed a handhold as the chopper was buffeted by a gust of wind. Although he wasn't supposed to start work until Monday, the station had brought him in a day early, with Tucker only too eager to agree if it meant his first trip ever in a helicopter. However, if the tinge of green in his face was any indication, the flight wasn't going nearly as smoothly as he had hoped.

"As you can see, folks," Tucker continued, swallowing hard, "with bad weather rolling in, Mother Nature may have the last word today. We'll keep updating you as the story develops."

"And cut!" his producer said. The moment the camera was off, Tucker dropped his mic, grabbed an air sickness bag, and heaved.

"Sorry," he said, wiping his mouth as the sour smell filled the tiny cabin, putting everyone else on board, which included his producer, his cameraman (Bill, who Tucker had taken to Channel 12 with him), and the pilot on the verge of following suit.

"What is it with that kid and grain elevators?" Bill muttered, holding his breath as he attempted to get a shot of Matt through the window while the chopper circled the elevator. "One of these days, he's going to get himself killed."

Bill's camera lens bumped up against the window as the chopper was hit by another gust. Tucker's hands shot out, one of them grabbing Bill's shoulder and the other a strap above his head. "Can we please set this thing down?" Tucker pleaded.

"Not until I get my shot," Bill said. "Now if you don't mind . . ." He nodded at his shoulder, prompting Tucker to release it.

§

Down on the ground, Chad, Dean, and Andrew shivered as they looked up at the circling helicopter.

"Man, if we're cold down here, imagine how Matt's feeling," Dean said, jumping up and down to warm himself as his teeth chattered. "I wonder if—"

"Wait," Chad said, grabbing his arm. "What's the sound?"

All three boys fell silent as they strained to hear anything beyond the helicopter's thumping blades. They didn't have to wait long. When the sound hit, they all recognized it immediately.

Thunder!

24

Too Close for Comfort

As he clung to his anchor ropes, his platform buffeted by the helicopter's downdraft and the gusting wind, there was no mistaking the flash of light on the horizon, or the rumble of thunder that followed. A thunderstorm was moving in, and fast. For Matt, that was the last straw. He'd made his point. There was no sense dying over it. It was time to come down.

He was about to grab his megaphone to announce his descent when a gust of wind kicked up and knocked it off the platform. Even though the megaphone, along with all his other gear, was tied to the platform, he must have tied a poor knot, because the megaphone broke loose and fell.

"Look out!" Matt cried, his voice swallowed almost immediately by the wind. He was thankful the police had created a perimeter below. Realizing his decision would become obvious once he started to climb down, Matt grabbed his coiled climbing rope and unfurled it over the edge, making sure to hold one end of it in his hand. However, the wind caught it as well, and before he realized what was happening, it whipped the rope out of his hand, sending it spiraling to the ground.

"No!" Matt cried. He sat back on the platform, suddenly queasy from looking over the edge. For the first time throughout his ordeal, he was truly scared. Without that rope, he had no way up or down. With no other options, he leaned his head over the edge of the platform.

"Help!"

§

Down on the ground, Romanowski and Constables Chambers and Rogers rushed in as soon as they saw the rope fall. Chambers grabbed one end of it and looked up. "Why do you think he did that?"

"I don't think he meant to," Romanowski said, barely able to hear Matt's faint calls for help over the wind. He picked up the smashed megaphone, examined it, and then looked up. "I think he's in trouble."

"How soon can that SWAT team get here?" Chambers asked. His words were followed almost immediately by a flash of lightning and a rumble of thunder, the first few drops of rain dotting his uniform.

"No time for that," Romanowski said, his mustache bristling as he thought through his options.

"What about the fire truck?" Chambers said. "They could pass the rope up to him."

"It's too windy," Romanowski said. "The thing could easily tip over. Besides, there's no way the kid can rappel down in this," he added as his cap nearly blew off his head.

"Then what?" Chambers asked, holding down his own cap in the wind. "Try getting at him from the top again?"

Romanowski shook his head as the sky was illuminated with another flash. "Too dangerous with all this lightning."

Just then he saw the Channel 12 chopper set down in an open area near the grain elevators. His eyes lit up. "Hey, I have an idea. Quick, coil up this rope."

§

Fearing it was only a matter of time before the wind tore his platform off the side of the elevator, all Matt could do was cling to his anchor ropes and pray they stayed in place.

"Why did I ever do this?" he wailed. "It's just a stupid grain elevator!"

Lightning flashed, and thunder crashed mere seconds afterward. Suddenly, the wind was the least of Matt's worries. For perhaps the first time he realized he had strapped himself to the tallest structure for miles around. If anything was going to get hit by lightning, it was the elevator. And if that happened . . .

He strained to look up and see if it had a lightning rod. Even if it did, would he be safe? What about the metal anchors that he had used to attach himself to the elevator? Would they attract lightning too?

"Help!" Matt cried as another bolt of lightning struck. "Somebody help me!"

As if in answer to his cries, he heard the thump of the chopper behind him. A few seconds later, it appeared from around the elevator. The side door was open, and Staff Sergeant Romanowski, who was strapped in, held up a megaphone as the pilot struggled to keep the machine level with Matt. "I've got your rope, kid. Do you have a climbing harness?"

Matt gave him a thumbs-up, realizing it would be useless to try to talk over the noise of the helicopter and the wind.

"Good. I'm going to lower the rope to you, and I want you to clip it onto your harness and un-clip yourself from the building. The minute you're ready, give us a signal, and we'll get you out of there. Wave your right hand if you understand."

Matt did as Romanowski instructed. Then the staff sergeant signaled to the pilot to ascend. Once he was high enough, Romanowski lowered the rope. It whipped and slashed in the wind, but Matt was finally able to snag it. His fingers half-frozen and his mind numb with fear, he ran the rope through his climbing harness and then secured it, tying three knots, just in case. Then, taking a deep breath, he unclipped himself from his anchor ropes, said a silent prayer, and indicated he was ready to go. He felt a brief tug as the rope tightened, and then the helicopter pulled him free of the elevator.

§

Down on the ground, Matt's parents, Chad, Joyce, Dean, Andrew, Mr. and Mrs. Muller, and Andrew's parents watched in a mixture of horror and amazement as Matt dangled from the bottom of the helicopter.

"I knew your boy was crazy, but I never knew he was this crazy!" Mrs. Muller said.

"Neither did we!" Mr. Taylor shouted over the wind.

Suddenly, a white ball of light exploded at the top of the elevator, followed by a thunderclap so loud that people cowered and screamed in fear. When they looked up again, they saw another flash of light, only this one was orange. The elevator had been hit, and it was on fire!

§

In an open field just east of town, the helicopter descended until Matt's feet touched the ground. He quickly unclipped himself, allowing the helicopter to swing over to the side and land several yards away. Matt stood up and dusted himself off, then looked back toward town.

"Oh my gosh," he said as he smoke billowing from the elevator's roof.

§

Within seconds the firemen leaped into action, connecting the hoses on their ladder truck to a nearby hydrant and calling in the town's second truck for backup. But with the wind still howling and lightning flashing, they didn't dare extend their ladder all the way, never mind send firemen up in it, lest they were struck by lightning too. The best they could do was operate the hose mounted on the ladder remotely from the ground, but it didn't come anywhere close to reaching the flames at the top of the elevator. The wind blew the powerful stream of water to the side like it was nothing but a garden hose.

§

Out in the field, Matt could hardly believe his eyes as Romanowski and the others came jogging up behind him. "Did I . . . did I do that?" Matt asked, his eyes glued to the flaming elevator.

Romanowski put a hand on his shoulder. "No, kid, but you're darn lucky we got you off that thing when we did."

Matt turned to look at him. "I know. You saved my life.

175

Thank you. All of you."

"We just did our job, kid," Romanowski said. "And now if you'll excuse me, my job's not over yet."

"I'll get an interview with you later!" Tucker said over his shoulder as he and Bill ran after the staff sergeant. "We need footage of this fire first!"

Not knowing what else to do, and still overwhelmed with shock at his near-death experience, Matt ran after them, already dreading the aftermath of the fire but worried even more about his parents' response to his ill-fated stunt.

25

A Surprising Offer

The following morning, not only the grain elevator but much of Milligan Creek's downtown core was a smoking ruin. The firefighters had fought valiantly, but the wind was so strong that it sent embers and flaming debris sailing toward Main Street. Rather than continue their fruitless battle against the blazing grain elevator, the firemen raced downtown, hoping to stop the fire from spreading. But even with two fire trucks on the scene and others brought in from nearby communities, they were soon overwhelmed. The flat tar-and-gravel roofs of multiple commercial buildings ignited, and the wind quickly fanned the flames into a roaring inferno. The best the firefighters could do was contain it. It was a nightmare the likes of which Milligan Creek had never seen before.

In the end, the only thing that saved the entire town from burning to the ground was a torrential downpour that finally allowed the firefighters to gain ground on the fire—that and a brief lull in the wind, which enabled a couple of water bombers stationed just north of Milligan Creek to fly over and douse the elevator and the downtown core with pink fire retardant.

Now, with the sun shining brightly, and hardly a breath of wind disturbing the smoke and steam that rose from the ruins, it was hard to believe the weather was responsible for the grim scene. Crowds of people lined the orange barricades as firemen continued to douse hot spots amongst piles of fallen timbers and cement blocks. Among the onlookers were Matt, Chad, Dean, and Andrew.

"I can't believe it," Matt said as they looked at the blackened remains of the town's sole hardware store.

"And I can't believe your parents let you out of the house after that stunt you pulled," Dean said. "If it were my parents, I don't think I'd see the sun again for at least twenty-five years."

"To be honest, I think they're too thankful I'm alive to be angry right now," Matt said. "Though I'm sure that won't last."

The boys all turned instinctively toward the empty patch of blue sky where the grain elevator had stood less than twenty-four hours earlier. "And to think we thought we could save it," Chad said.

"Yeah, I guess Mother Nature had other plans," Dean replied.

Matt squinted in the early morning sun. "If I didn't know better, I'd say Fortitude planned that storm."

Andrew nodded. "It certainly made their job easier."

"Look on the bright side," Dean said. "At least one of their elevators is still here." Thankfully, the wind had blown the embers away from the other two elevators, sparing them from destruction.

"If only there was a town to go with it," Matt said, turning back toward the wreckage in front of them.

§

At school the following day, the mood was decidedly subdued. The administration had even brought in grief counselors to help students who were traumatized by the devastation. And Mayor Bondar spoke to them at a special assembly, promising that no matter how bad things looked, the town would rebuild, making it bigger, stronger, and better than ever.

Despite his ordeal and the loss of the grain elevator, Matt felt surprisingly good, his spirits buoyed in no small part by his newfound celebrity status. Tucker's story on the fire, including Matt's protest and dramatic rescue, had been picked up by news outlets across the country and even internationally, putting Milligan Creek on the map in a way that none of the boys could have anticipated. Staff Sergeant Romanowski was being hailed as a hero. The story had even prompted an investigation into the way Fortitude conducted business, with critics accusing them of using strong-arm tactics to force small towns across the prairies to bend to their will.

As the boys passed through the gym at noon hour on their way to the lunch room, Matt heard someone call his name. It was Mr. Karky, and he did not look happy, though he seldom did. He motioned Matt over to his office. "Get in here, Taylor. I want to talk to you."

Matt swallowed hard. He knew he was about to get in trouble. Big trouble. Not only had he "borrowed" the climbing harness he used for his stunt, the rope was school property too. Even though he had returned them both, he was certain Karky had a suitable punishment in mind.

"See you later, guys," Matt said as he set off toward Mr. Karky's office. "I hope."

"Good luck," Chad said.

"Have a seat," Mr. Karky said as Matt entered. "And close the door behind you, please."

Matt felt uneasy suddenly. Usually, Mr. Karky disciplined students by having them stand in front of his desk while he yelled at them for fifteen minutes straight, then doled out an appropriate punishment. However, not only was Mr. Karky breaking with tradition by asking Matt to sit down, he had used the word "please," which Matt didn't realize was in Mr. Karky's vocabulary. That couldn't be good.

"Quite the stunt you pulled this weekend, Taylor."

Matt lowered his eyes. "Yes, sir."

"Nearly got yourself killed."

"I know, sir."

"I'll bet your parents were worried sick."

Matt nodded.

"Well, contrary to what you may believe, I didn't call you in here to punish you."

Matt looked up, meeting Mr. Karky's gaze. "You didn't?"

The gym teacher shook his head. "No, but I could have you polishing my gym floor for the rest of the year due to your gross misuse, not to mention misappropriation, of school property." The familiar anger rose momentarily in his brown eyes. "But I called you in for another reason—to announce my retirement."

Matt gave him a puzzled look. "Excuse me?"

"I'd also like to offer you a job."

Matt sat back in his chair, suddenly wondering if he was still in shock from the weekend's incident and having delusions as well. He shook his head slowly. "I'm sorry, sir, but I don't think I understand."

"You like climbing, right?"

"Yes."

"And grain elevators?"

"Yes, but—"

"Good. Then you're hired."

Matt almost had to laugh. "I'm sorry, Mr. Karky, but none of this makes any sense."

"Maybe this'll help." Mr. Karky unfurled a hand-drawn sketch on his desk. It featured a picture of a grain elevator with the words "Karky's Klimbing Gym" on it.

Matt shook his head slowly as he stared at it. "I still don't understand, sir."

"You're looking at the new owner of the one Fortitude grain elevator you didn't manage to burn down."

Matt looked up from the drawing. "You bought the other elevator?"

"Yep. While everyone was out there gawking at the fire, I was on the phone with Fortitude, and they sold it to me for a song. All I have to do is move it, and I already have a company lined up to do that. Then I'm going to take early retirement from teaching and turn it into an indoor/outdoor climbing gym. If all goes well, I'll have it up and running by next summer.

"Think about it, Taylor. People love grain elevators, and with more and more of them disappearing, my gym is going to turn into a major tourist attraction. Climbers are going to flock to it from across the country—maybe even from across the world. All thanks to you and your stupid stunt. It was the best free publicity a guy could hope for. Seeing as your crazy antics gave me the idea, I figured the least I could do is offer you a job. So, what do you say?"

"I don't know, I—"

"Just say yes, Taylor."

"Yes!" Matt smiled and shook Mr. Karky's outstretched hand. And for perhaps the first time ever, he saw Mr. Karky smile.

26

A New Beginning

After school that day, Matt and Chad burst in the door to their home, Dean and Andrew right behind them. "Mom, Dad, you'll never guess what happened today," Matt said. "Mr. Karky—" He pulled up short when he saw his parents' grim faces. His heart nearly stopped when he realized they were seated at the kitchen table alongside Dean's parents, Mr. and Mrs. Muller; and Andrew's parents, Mr. and Mrs. Loewen. Matt swallowed hard. "Is . . . is something wrong?"

Mrs. Taylor patted the chair beside her. "Sit down. All of you."

The boys did as she instructed, all four of them dreading what was to come, though none of them more so than Matt.

"What you did this weekend was foolish, Matt," Mrs. Taylor began.

"Not to mention dangerous," Mr. Taylor added, giving Matt a stern look.

"And despite your protests to the contrary, we know you didn't act alone," Mrs. Muller said, narrowing her eyes at Dean. He hung his head, as did the other boys.

"We've been sitting here all afternoon trying to come up with a suitable punishment," Mrs. Taylor continued.

"And trust me, we've had no shortage of good ideas," Mrs. Muller remarked.

"But it seems like the first part of our plan has already come to fruition," Mrs. Taylor said.

Matt looked up at her. "What do you mean?"

"You were going to tell us about Mr. Karky. He offered you the job?"

"Yes," Matt said, "but how did you—"

"Seeing as you boys were all so eager to volunteer your time on behalf of Mayor Bondar, we thought you'd be willing to do the same for others," Mr. Taylor said. "Starting with Mr. Karky."

Matt shook his head. "But he didn't say anything about volunteering."

"Maybe not, but that's what you're going to be—for starters," Mr. Taylor said. "You can talk about a wage once you've repaid your debt to society."

"How long is that?" Matt asked, sinking into his seat.

"We'll leave that to Mr. Karky to decide," Mr. Taylor said.

"No wonder he was smiling," Matt mumbled.

"As for the rest of you," Mr. Muller said, "we figured some community service might also give you a little . . . fortitude, if you'll pardon the expression."

"Doing what?" Dean asked, a kernel of fear growing in his stomach as he looked up at the adults' smiling faces.

"Oh, you're going to love this," Mrs. Muller said, rubbing her hands together in gleeful anticipation.

Seven months later at the crack of dawn, Andrew's dad pulled to a stop on the west side of town. Chad, Dean, and Andrew were crammed into his truck cab beside him.

"I can't believe Matt gets to work in Karky's climbing gym, and we have to do this," Dean said, opening the door. He shivered as a blast of cold April wind hit him. "We're going to freeze to death out here."

"Not if you work fast," Mr. Loewen said. "That'll heat you up. Besides, it'll get warmer once the sun comes up."

"Yeah, it might actually get above zero degrees," Dean grumbled.

The boys piled out of the truck and stood and faced the construction site. The green Fortitude logo was everywhere. "I can't believe it," Chad said as he watched an army of men and machines prepare to break ground on construction of the new inland grain terminal. "Our worst nightmare come true, and now we have to play a part in making it happen."

"You mean *my* worst nightmare," a voice from behind them said. They all whirled to see Matt wearing a hard hat with the Fortitude logo on the front. In his hands were three more hard hats and three pairs of work gloves, which he passed out to the other boys. "You didn't think I was going to leave you guys to work out here on your own, did you?"

"What about Mr. Karky?" Andrew asked as he put on his hard hat, then took it off to adjust the fit.

"He figured a few early mornings out in the cold would be good for me, toughen me up."

Andrew nodded. "That sounds like him."

185

Once the others were suited up, Matt clapped his hands together, the thick leather work gloves making a thumping noise in the cool morning air. "So, boys, are you ready to make history?"

"Don't you mean embrace the future?" Dean asked.

Matt looked out at the construction site and sighed. "I guess so."

Chad clapped him on the shoulder. "Cheer up, bro. We may have lost our grain elevators, but despite your best efforts, we may have just saved our town."

"That and Mayor Bondar's going ahead with our pet cemetery idea," Andrew said. "Imagine that."

Dean's face went white. "Are you serious? Does he have any idea what kind of horrors that could unleash?"

The other boys laughed. Dean really did need to upgrade his reading material.

A Brief Note on the Inspiration Behind This Book

People often ask me if any of the characters in my books represent me. The truth is, they all do to some extent. But in this book, Matt comes closest to how I approach life.

Like most people, I'm a bundle of contradictions. I love innovation and technology, but I hate change. I want everything to remain just the way I remember it. Especially the places I knew growing up. But as Mayor Bondar points out in this book, change is the only constant, and if we don't adapt to it we'll die, or at least be left behind.

Foam Lake has had to embrace a lot of change. When I was the same age as the boys in this book, way back in 1985, the annex on one of the town's grain elevators caught fire, burning it to the ground. Worse, the ashes spread, igniting fires that consumed some businesses downtown.

Twenty-one years later, Foam Lake was hit with two more fires within the space of a month. One burned several more businesses, and the other destroyed one of the town's grain elevators and ignited the other. Like it or not, Foam Lake had changed. But the people who lived there adapted, and today the community continues to thrive.

Apart from these catastrophes, in many ways Foam Lake is much the way I remember it. Certain aspects of the town have changed, but so have I. I tend to see the changes in myself as a good thing, so I guess I should feel the same way about other changes in life. But I can't deny the pang of sadness I feel every time I drive past an old, abandoned grain elevator and remember days gone by.

Despite all the other changes in life, that's one feeling that I'm certain will always remain the same.

About the Author

Kevin Miller grew up on a farm outside of Foam Lake, Saskatchewan, where he dreamed of becoming a writer. He got his first break as a newspaper reporter in Meadow Lake, SK. Within a year, he parlayed that into a job in book publishing, which eventually enabled him to become a full-time freelance writer and editor.

From there, Kevin transitioned into film, and he spent the next thirteen years traveling the world while working on a variety of feature films, documentaries, and short film projects. In addition to serving as a screenwriter, he has also worked as a director, producer, and film editor. These days, Kevin splits his time between writing, editing, filmmaking, and teaching.

When he's not working, he enjoys hanging out with his wife and four kids, fishing, hiking, canoeing, skiing, playing hockey, skateboarding, and otherwise exploring his world.

Kevin likes to talk about books, movies, and writing almost as much as he enjoys writing. If you'd like to contact Kevin about any of these topics, to tell him what you think of his novels, or to book him for a speaking engagement, you can reach him at www.kevinmillerxi.com.

Up the Creek!

When best friends Matt, Chad, Dean, and Andrew set out on a canoe trip down Milligan Creek during spring run-off season, little do they realize that their voyage through small-town Saskatchewan is about to turn into one of the wildest experiences of their lives—if they survive!

Unlimited

A school field trip to the local Wetlands Unlimited marsh just outside of Milligan Creek, SK, gives Matt, Chad, Dean, and Andrew a brilliant idea: hijacking the radio signal that transmits a recorded message about the marsh and using it to launch their own pirate radio station. Broadcasting late at night, mostly for their own amusement, their show quickly becomes an underground sensation. Keeping their identities a secret, the boys are ecstatic about the growing popularity of their program, until it draws the attention of Wetlands Unlimited—and the police!

The Water War

When a beautiful, mysterious new girl moves to Milligan Creek, everyone in town is so smitten that her mere presence threatens to ruin the perfect summer that Matt has planned for him, his brother, Chad, and their best friends, Andrew and Dean. So, the boys come up with what seems like the perfect distraction: a water war. It's the ultimate game of survival, where every player is both hunter and prey. But when Matt's buddies invite the new girl to join in, the game that was supposed to unite them against the interloper threatens to tear their close friendship apart.

Snowbound!

When a number of mysterious snow tunnels begin to show up in the ditches around the small town of Milligan Creek, Matt and Chad Taylor and their best friends, Dean and Andrew ,are determined to figure out who is making them and why. As they hunt for the person responsible, the mysterious tunnels and that winter's record snowfall inspires them to create their own epic snow maze, to which they plan to charge admission. However, with a once-in-a-century blizzard forecast to hit the prairies, the race is on to solve the mystery and complete their maze before the entire province is covered in a glistening blanket of white.

For more details, visit www.kevinmillerxi.com.

Made in the USA
Coppell, TX
10 January 2021

47882791R00105